TURTLE TIME

Other Avon Camelot Books by
Jeanne Betancourt

THE RAINBOW KID

Other Avon Flare Books by
Jeanne Betancourt

AM I NORMAL?
DEAR DIARY

JEANNE BETANCOURT is the author of the award-winning book, SMILE: HOW TO COPE WITH BRACES. Her other books include AM I NORMAL?, DEAR DIARY, THE EDGE, and THE RAINBOW KID.

She also writes screenplays and television scripts, including ''I Want to Go Home,'' an ABC After School Special.

Jeanne Betancourt lives in New York City and Connecticut with her husband, her teenage daughter, a cat, and a dog.

TURTLE TIME

Jeanne Betancourt

AN AVON CAMELOT BOOK

TURTLE TIME is an original publication of Avon Books. This work has never before appeared in book form.

AVON BOOKS
A division of
The Hearst Corporation
1790 Broadway
New York, New York 10019

Copyright © 1985 by Jeanne Betancourt
Published by arrangement with the author
Library of Congress Catalog Card Number: 84-045678
ISBN: 0-380-89675-3

First Camelot Printing, June 1985

CAMELOT TRADEMARK REG. U. S. PAT. OFF. AND IN
OTHER COUNTRIES, MARCA REGISTRADA, HECHO EN
U. S. A.

Printed in the U. S. A.

OPB 10 9 8 7 6 5 4 3 2 1

For John Gilmour

CHAPTER ONE

THE FRIDAY BEFORE SCHOOL STARTED MY MOM TOOK ME shopping for school clothes and stationery supplies. I got loads of stuff. By the time we finished we were starving. So we stopped at Chez Michele's for supper before I went back to Dad's.

My mom smiled at me over her chef salad. She was nervous about something. Why else would she be tearing a lettuce leaf into itsy-bitsy pieces and piling them in a pyramid on the restaurant's pink table cloth?

"So it's back to the old grind in a few days," she said. "I guess you'll miss Sister Bernard Marie."

"Uh-huh. She was neat." Sister Bernard Marie, last year's teacher, was an old-fashioned nun with a long black habit and clinking rosary beads—not a modern nun in a suit. And she was nice as could be.

Mom smiled that nervous smile again. "Things change. Who knows, you might end up liking your new teacher as much as Sister Bernard Marie. Maybe even more."

I chewed on a big bite of my cheeseburger and shook my head to say "no way."

"You might be surprised. That is if you're willing to give the new person a chance." Now she was pulling the little seeds from a piece of cucumber and laying them out in a neat row around the edge of her butter dish, skipping the spots where there were painted roses. "Which reminds me. There's uh . . . uh . . . there's something I've been meaning to tell you, Aviva."

I took a sip of my Shirley Temple. "What's up, Mom?"

7

She looked me straight in the eye and said, "George is going to move in with us."

"What?" I screamed. "No way!"

The people at the next table turned to look at us. I leaned forward and lowered my voice. "Are you getting married or something?"

She laughed nervously. "No. No. It's just that we spend so much time together it seems silly to keep two places. One of them is almost always empty."

"Does Dad know?" I asked.

"It shouldn't make any difference to him. But of course I'll tell him."

Mom chattered on, telling me how handy it would be to have a man around the house and how special George was. That sort of thing.

George did spend a lot of time with us and the truth was he wasn't *so* bad. But to live with us? That was different. That meant he'd never go home. He'd always *be* home. In my home.

"You'll get used to it, honey. All things considered, you two get along pretty well. George thinks you're very special."

I knew she wanted me to say, "He's special too—I like him." But I didn't. Instead I said, "What about Cindy?"

Cindy is George's daughter from *his* first marriage. If George gave up his apartment, where would Cindy stay during her college holidays? We only had two bedrooms.

"Well, she'll stay at our place, of course," Mom said. "Besides, you live with Dad every other week, so it shouldn't affect you that much."

"Where will she sleep when she's there? Not in my room."

Mom looked at me coolly. "Why don't we take one step at a time. George is moving in this weekend. You start school on Monday. I think there's enough going on without worrying about where Cindy will sleep. Now let's get the check and I'll bring you back to your dad's."

Since my parents got divorced last year I've lived one week with my mom in our old house, then one week with my dad in his new apartment. Back and forth, back and forth. My old English sheepdog, Mop, went with me until Dad's crummy landlord said, "No dogs allowed." This was a Mopless Dad week.

My mother had hardly eaten her salad. All she'd done was play with it. "Mom, why don't you have them put the salad in a doggie bag," I suggested.

She looked at it. "Mop doesn't eat salad."

"Not for Mop. For you—later."

The waitress stood over us. "Dessert, ladies? We have a special hot fudge sundae tonight."

"Do you want one?" Mom asked me.

"Do you?" I asked back.

"Why not?" she said.

"Two hot fudge sundaes, a cup of coffee, and a salad bag for the doggie," Mom said. "I mean a doggie bag for the salad. Please."

Even when your mother's boyfriend is moving into your house a hot fudge sundae tastes pretty good.

Besides, we both eat chocolate when we're upset.

CHAPTER TWO

Dad	Mom	Mom	Mom	Mom	Mom	Mom
	School Starts					
S 11	M 12	T 13	W 14	Th 15	F 16	S 17

THE FIRST DAY OF SCHOOL IS ALWAYS EXCITING. I LOVE SEE-
ing how everyone's changed and gotten bigger and
what new clothes they got. We were wandering around
our new classroom saying, ''So how was your summer?'' And ''I love your new jacket.'' And ''Did you see
such and such a movie?'' And ''Gee, I wonder who the
new teacher will be?''

Then HE came into the room.

I don't know how he got through the doorway
without ducking. That's how tall Mr. Jackson was.

The noise in the room dropped to a jittery mumble
as he walked over to the blackboard and wrote in neat
letters, *M-r. J-a-c-k-s-o-n*. He turned around and silently
looked us over. I tried not to stare, but he was a *big* black
man, sort of like Mr. T with hair. His neck was as thick
as a tree trunk and he had the biggest hands ever. I figured he had more muscles in his baby finger than Josh
Greene had in his whole body.

We moved around the room, trying to get seats next
to our best friends. Mr. Jackson boomed, ''Ladies and
gentlemen, freeze!''

The room fell dead silent. We froze in position—like
we were playing a game of statues. I froze as I was tight-
ening the rubber band around my ponytail by splitting it
in half and tugging. I stood there with my arms up in the

air—like I was being arrested. In each raised hand I held a long wad of dark hair.

"Kindly line up along the side of the room. One behind the other." I dropped my arms and followed Sue.

Mr. Jackson put his hands behind his back as he watched us.

"Face front."

We did.

"If you cannot see over the head of the person in front of you, move up one."

We did.

"This is silly," someone behind me whispered.

"Mr. Cioffi," Mr. J. said in a deep, rumbling voice.

Cioffi said, "How'd you know my name? I mean, I didn't say nothin'."

" 'I didn't say *anything*, Mr. Jackson.' Kindly write that on the front left blackboard twenty times while the rest of the class receive their seat assignments."

Everyone held their breath. Cioffi opened his mouth to talk back, which is what you'd expect from Cioffi. Josh nudged him and he wisely closed it. Josh Greene is no dummy.

Mr. J. looked at us sternly. "Ladies and gentlemen, continue." People kept moving in front of me and I kept moving back. I'd been the tallest girl in my class since nursery school. Josh moved to the end of the line without even checking to see how tall everyone else was. The only sound in the room was the scratching of Cioffi's chalk on the blackboard and the shuffle of our feet. By the time we were done Sue was the first in line and Josh was the last, right behind me.

"Double-check to be sure the person in front of you is shorter than you are," Mr. J. said.

Janet raised her hand.

"Yes, Miss Saunders?" He knew her name too! How could he? He was brand new to the school.

"Mr. Jackson," Janet said in her primmest voice. "Do shoes count? Because I'm standing in front of Rita, but she has on cowboy heels and I have on flats. I know for a fact that I'm at least—"

"Miss Saunders, disregard the shoes. Stay where you are."

Mr. J. looked at the back of the line. "Mr. Greene, are you quite certain that you can see over Miss Granger's head?" He knew *everybody's* name.

"Sure."

" 'Yes, Mr. Jackson. I believe I can,' would be the correct way to answer. That is, if you were correct, Mr. Greene. As it is you are *in*correct. Miss Granger is clearly an inch taller than you are."

Everyone turned around and stared at us.

"That's because she has on—"

"Mr. Greene, kindly change places with Miss Granger."

"Cheat," Josh mumbled as he moved in front of me.

Truth was I had on sneakers, just like Josh. So I wasn't the tallest girl in the class anymore. I was the tallest kid in the class.

While Mr. Jackson was assigning seats to the kids in front of me I couldn't take my eyes off the army green knapsack slung over Josh's right shoulder. First of all I'd never seen Josh with a bookbag—of any kind. Secondly when Josh was standing perfectly still, the bookbag . . . *jumped.*

When we got to our assigned seats in the back of

the room I watched as Josh carefully hung his knapsack over the back of his chair. I stared at it. Nothing. I must have imagined it. Then—sure enough—it moved again!

While Mr. J. was putting some math problems on the board I leaned over and poked Josh. "What's in there?" I mouthed silently as I pointed to his knapsack. He shrugged.

"Miss Granger," Mr. J. said without turning away from the board. "If you have something to say to Mr. Greene save it until after school."

No one laughed. We were in shock. Who could believe it? Mr. Jackson not only knew everyone's last name, but he also had eyes in the back of his head. That was when we knew for sure that seventh grade was going to be a nightmare. Our only relief would be English with Sister Bernard Marie at two o'clock and Music with old Sister Mary Rose on Friday afternoons. Mr. J. was our everything-else teacher, including Gym.

Lunchtime couldn't come soon enough.

"He looks like an ex-convict to me," said Rita as she munched on a carrot.

"Or a boxer. Maybe he's a retired boxer," said Janet. "Heavyweight division."

I said, "I think he was a Marine sergeant."

"Who murdered someone and now he's doing good works to repent for his sins," Sue added.

When we got back to the classroom from lunch, Mr. J. was already putting History questions on the board. We just went to our places—silently. There was a note on my desk.

ROSES R RED

VIOLETS R BLUE

SINCE MYRTLE HID

IN MY GRANDMA'S BED

WE DECIDED

2 GIVE HER 2 U

P.S. WHEN U LOOK

IN YOUR DESK DON'T

SCREAM

I looked over at Josh. What now? He was studying the blackboard and began to copy the questions with the pencil he'd borrowed from me on the paper he'd borrowed from me. His knapsack hung empty and limp over the back of his chair.

I took a deep breath, slowly lifted my desk top, looked inside and swallowed the biggest scream of my life.

Filling at least half of the space inside my desk was a greenish brown turtle with a snaky, slimy speckled head. It blinked its beady yellow eyes at me and pulled back under the shell with a hiss.

I banged my desk closed.

Mr. Jackson gave a little jump and then without turning said, "Do try to be quieter, Miss Granger."

Josh covered a grin with his hand and looked straight ahead.

I didn't open my desk for the rest of the day.

"You can't just leave it there," I told Josh when we were finally released from Jackson Jail.

"You're the one who left her."

It was strange to be talking to Josh after the long summer. I was taller than he was now. But he had changed, too. He looked older and skinnier than I remembered. He had on new jeans (that was nice) and a sweatshirt that said, "Sweet Horizons Cemetery." He leaned against the school building and stuck his hands in his pockets. "Myrtle's yours now." He smiled. "She's not just any turtle, you know. She's special."

"To you she's special. To me she's disgusting."

"I've had her all summer," he said. "She's a Diamondback Terrapin, you know. They're very rare. It's a

15

privilege to have one. I can tell you all about her. What to feed her. Everything.''

"If she's so special why don't you keep her?''

"She got under my grandmother's sheets and scared her, so I have to get rid of her. Didn't you read the note?''

"My dog doesn't want a turtle around,'' I answered.

"So leave her at your dad's.'' He slid his back along the school building and sat down. I leaned over so he'd have to look at me. "No pets allowed. Remember?''

"A turtle? Give me a break. You have to do better than that. Besides, I'm not really giving her to you. I'm asking you to take care of her until I get a place of my own.''

"A place of your own? You're only twelve years old!''

"Turtles live a long time. Hundreds of years. I'll be through high school in six years. I'm sure I can take a turtle to veterinary school. Six years is nothing to a turtle.''

"Well six years is a lot to me. That's half of my life so far.''

"Look, your mom pays me for walking Mop when you're at your dad's. Right?''

"Yeah. That's right.''

"So I'll pay you for taking care of Myrtle. It'll be your job. Two bucks a week.''

Money. That was something to consider. "Make it two fifty.''

"Two twenty-five.''

"Every week or just the weeks you walk Mop?''

"Every week.''

"Okay. On a trial basis. But you get it out of my desk. I'm not touching it until we've been introduced."

He slid back up the building and grinned. "It's a deal. You'll see. You'll like having a turtle. To know Myrtle is to love her."

I walked the mile home with Myrtle in Josh's knapsack over one shoulder and my bookbag over the other. When I reached our block I saw a blue Volkswagen in the driveway. George's. I'd forgotten. George moved in while I was at Dad's. But what was he doing there now? Didn't he go to work, for goodness sakes?

I unlocked the kitchen door and went in. Mop met me with barks and licks and jumps.

"Hi there," George yelled from the living room. I dropped my bookbag on the kitchen floor and went over to the doorway between the kitchen and living room.

There he sat, wrapped in a plaid bathrobe, in my dad's old easy chair that was now *my* old easy chair. Violin music was playing on the stereo, and the living room looked like a garage sale. Clutter everywhere. Boxes of books and records. Extra chairs that we didn't need. Bookshelves that didn't even match the ones we had. A chrome-and-glass coffee table that looked stupid in our comfy old-fashioned place. And worst of all, a big yarn rug in my least favorite color—puke green.

"So," George said through a sniffle, "here I am home with a cold."

Home?

He smiled a weak sick-person smile. "How you doing, Aviva?"

I didn't answer. I just stood there. In shock. Mop licked my fingers and sniffed around me. Myrtle shifted in the knapsack. That's when Mop went crazy. He got a

17

whiff of Myrtle and barked and jumped on me, trying to get to the knapsack. What if he knocked me over and I fell on Myrtle?

I screamed to George. "Quick! There's a turtle on my back."

It took him forever, but he finally got the idea. "Throw me the turtle and grab Mop," he shouted as he squatted in a kind of quarterback position to catch Myrtle.

How do you throw a ten-pound turtle? Carefully.

I threw Myrtle.

George caught Myrtle.

And I grabbed Mop by the collar.

When Mop and I got back from his walk George was in my easy chair again, drinking orange juice and watching the all-news cable channel. Myrtle was in the bathroom doing what all turtles do. Not much.

I went to the kitchen to get my regular after-school snack of graham crackers with peanut butter and Marshmallow Fluff and a glass of milk. Only I used twice as much Marshmallow Fluff as usual and ate standing in the kitchen instead of sitting in my favorite easy chair watching my four-thirty soap opera.

The phone rang. My mom. I forgot to give her my after-school call at work to say yes I'm all right and no I wasn't mugged on the way home from school.

I started to tell her about Mr. Jackson and Myrtle.

George came into the kitchen and said, "If it's Janet I want to talk to her." He just stood there waiting for me to finish talking to my mother.

I stopped dead in the middle of what I was saying and told her George wanted to talk to her.

She didn't even care that I hadn't finished what I

was saying. "Oh, dear," she said. "George? Is he all right? What's he doing home?"

Home?

"Ask him," I muttered as I handed the phone to George.

Mop and I went to my room and did a little bit of what Myrtle does. Not much.

When Mom first saw Myrtle she said, "*Yuck*. Disgusting. Get that creature out of here." Which is exactly what I was thinking about George.

I explained that Josh's grandmother wouldn't let him keep it and that Myrtle would stay at Dad's. Mom said, "Poor Josh. He doesn't have a very good home life. He's really such a nice boy." She squatted down and studied Myrtle more closely. They looked into each other's eyes. Mom laughed out loud, which caused Myrtle to go back in her shell with a hiss. "I'd just love to see your father's face when you bring this thing to live in his nice modern apartment."

After supper George went to bed with his cold and I helped Mom unpack some of his boxes so I could use an empty one for Myrtle. We finally started on the box I had my eye on. It was at least four feet square and was labeled in big red magic marker, "Pots, Pans, Spices, Etc." The Etc. was five boxes of half-eaten cereal and two boxes of prunes. I looked at all the stuff in the box. Now we'd have two toasters and two popcorn makers at Mom's and none at Dad's. Divorce is not very practical.

That night Myrtle stayed in the living room and Mop stayed with me. The trick was to always keep them separate, with one of them behind a closed door. When I left for school Myrtle's box was in my bedroom, and

Mop was sniffing along the bottom door edge. That's what Mop was doing when I got home from school every day that week.

On Friday my mom got home from work before George. I followed her into her bedroom and sat cross-legged in the middle of her bed. I looked around. George's clothes were everywhere. He must have had ten thousand pairs of shoes and sneakers lying around —all old. It didn't smell like Mom's room anymore. Maybe because of the shoes.

I fiddled with the edge of Mom's quilt while she changed from her work dress to her sweatshirt and jeans. "What's up?" she asked as she brushed her short brown hair with her fingers.

I assumed a very serious tone and said what I'd practiced all the way home from school. "George is all right and it's nice you have a boyfriend, but it would be better if he had his own place."

She looked at me from her dresser mirror. "Well I don't like Myrtle living here. Maybe Myrtle should get her own place."

"That's silly and you know it. Besides, Myrtle's moving out when I go to Dad's next week."

"And George is not moving out," she said in her there's-no-room-for-discussion voice.

Just then the kitchen door shut closed. There he was. George. Here to stay. Not here today, gone tomorrow—like Myrtle.

The next morning I claimed my easy chair while George was taking his shower. I rolled the TV closer and turned on the Mr. T cartoon. My friends and I had vowed to watch Mr. T so we could compare him with Mr. J. As Mr. T filled the screen I tried to picture him with even darker skin, black curly hair, and dressed in a suit and tie. (Mr. J. wore a suit and tie every day. Louise said that his clothes were so neat because he had a white valet to take care of his every need—like a bodyguard. I said no way does Mr. J. need a bodyguard—we do.)

Actually I get pretty bored with cartoons now that I'm in the seventh grade. What I really wish is they'd have soap operas on Saturday morning. Or reruns of the best soap operas from the whole week before. Different ones on different channels so you could go from one to the other and find out what you missed during the week when you had to go to the orthodontist or something.

I was thinking about this when the front door bell rang. I went to see who it was.

It was Josh Greene. He shifted nervously from one foot to the other. "I was over this way so I thought I'd check up on Myrtle and give you some tips on how to take care of her."

Mop pushed past me and started barking excitedly and jumping all over Josh, licking his face and everything. Josh walks Mop after school the weeks I go to my Dad's, so I'd never seen Mop and Josh together before.

Josh and Mop followed me into the living room. Mop was going crazy with excitement. He pushed Josh over. They rolled around the floor, loving each other up. As I watched them I wondered, if Mop had to choose which one of us he loved better, who would he choose?

Finally I spoke up. "Are you here to play with Mop or to tell me about Myrtle? I have other things to do, you know."

Josh put his arm around Mop's neck and they both sat there on George's puke green rug, staring at me.

This is how I felt watching Mop snuggle up to Josh. Very jealous.

"Have they met?" Josh asked.

"Have who met?"

"Mop and Myrtle."

Just then Mop pulled away from Josh and came over and licked my hand. Mop is a smart, sensitive dog, but I hate pity. I put my arm around his neck and rubbed behind his ears to calm him down.

I said, "Don't you like your turtle or something? Mop could hurt it, you know."

"Mop and Myrtle will get along fine," Josh insisted.

"If you'd seen how Mop behaved when I came in with Myrtle you'd know what I was talking about." Josh Greene could be such a know-it-all. "Have you ever seen a dog and a turtle together?" I asked.

He got up off the rug. "No, but I'm going to."

Just then George came out of the shower in an old red terry cloth bathrobe and *my* Garfield cat towel around his neck.

"Hi, Mr. O'Connell," Josh said. How'd he know George? Josh was getting to be like Mr. J.

George rubbed the water out of his eyes with the end of the towel and squinted through the sun shining in the living room. "Josh!" He came into the living room to shake Josh's hand and slap him on the back. "Josh. Great to see you. How've you been?"

The kitchen door banged. Mom was back with our groceries. She yelled from the kitchen, "Is that Josh Greene?" She came into the living room without even putting down her shopping bag. "Well, well. Am I glad to see you. I want to hear all about school and how you've been."

Josh sort of smiled at my mom and let out a deep breath. I could tell they really liked each other. "School's awful and I'm fine," he said. "I came to make sure Myrtle's all right and introduce her to Mop."

I reminded them I was there too. "Dogs and turtles don't get along. Everybody knows that."

"Let's see," said Josh.

Twenty minutes later Mop and Myrtle were lying side by side in a patch of sun in the living room. Every few seconds Mop would open an eye and check on what Myrtle was doing. Which, of course, was nothing. Once he was convinced that that was all Myrtle was going to do, Mop joined us in the kitchen. Mom, Josh, me . . . and George . . . had grilled cheese and tomato sandwiches for lunch. Josh had three sandwiches and practically a whole quart of milk. I think he was trying to get as tall as me. Who cares?

Mom, George, and Josh had a great old time. George told Josh what it was like to grow up on a farm and all the times the local veterinarian saved the animals' lives. Josh said he thought he'd rather be a country vet who took care of farm animals and got to be outdoors a lot than a city vet who took care of poodles with ribbons in their hair.

I couldn't wait until he left.

CHAPTER THREE

Mom	Dad	Dad	Dad	Dad	Dad	Dad
						Sue's sleep over
S 18	M 19	T 20	W 21	Th 22	F 23	S 24

"A TURTLE? SURE, HONEY. THAT'LL BE NICE," MY DAD SAID when I told him that I had a job taking care of a turtle. "You just leave it in a little box with your suitcase at the front door, and I'll get it when I pick up your other things after work tomorrow."

Then I told him how Mr. Jackson had given us a ridiculous amount of homework and some other stuff about school. As we were saying good-bye Dad brought up Myrtle again. "You know we can keep the turtle in one of those pretty little round goldfish bowls. Maybe put it on the coffee table."

After I hung up the phone I went looking for Myrtle. I found her in the kitchen, slowly crawling across the black and white tiles toward the last patch of sun. Mop was crouched under the table keeping an eye on her every move. Little fish bowl? Coffee table? She filled one of the twelve-inch square tiles that covered our kitchen floor. Why, she was about half the size of Dad's coffee table. I decided Dad was thinking about a different kind of turtle.

The first thing I did when I got to Dad's after school on Monday was check out the refrigerator. I figured I'd surprise him by making supper—to make up a little for Myrtle's size.

This is what was in the refrigerator:

24

2 pieces of pizza half-wrapped in aluminum foil
  from the last time I was at Dad's
3 apricot yogurts
½ head of lettuce
some butter
a little milk
4 diet sodas

I closed the door and checked my watch. Three forty-five. My soap opera started at four-thirty. If I rushed I could pick up the groceries and cook supper and set the table while I watched my soap opera. Dinner would be ready when Dad walked in—with Myrtle.

We have a charge account at the grocery store so I shopped for the week—another surprise for Dad. This is what I cooked while Jason told Eleanor that he knew all along that their child was really Louis's, and Eleanor told Louis that his mother's deadly lung disease was caused by the pollution from *his* factory: noodles with melted cheese, broccoli, and chocolate pudding.

By the time Dad's key was turning in the door the macaroni-and-cheese casserole was in the oven, the TV was back in my room, the table in the living room was set (with candles), and I was curled up on the couch reading my History homework.

"Aviva!" he shouted as he came through the door. "Where are you?" Then he saw me—his darling little girl, whom he hadn't seen in a week, doing her homework. His glance took in the graciously set table, his nose the aroma of my home-cooked meal. He put down my suitcase, dragged in Myrtle's box, and screamed, "Aviva Granger, this isn't a turtle. It's a prehistoric beast!" He pointed at the box. "Is this . . . thing . . . supposed to be a joke or something?"

25

I calmly got up from my cozy spot on the couch and went over to kiss him hello and say what *he* always says when I'm unhappy about something. "You're all worked up. Let's have a nice dinner and talk about it over dessert. Chocolate pudding."

During dinner I kept the chatter going by bringing Dad up to date on Mr. J. and Josh. I got him to tell me about his new classes at the college. Dad was looking pretty relaxed when the doorbell rang. We looked at each other. Who could it be? Dad hit his forehead with the heel of his hand. "Oh, no. I ordered Chinese take-out before I left school!" He checked his watch. "And told them to deliver it at six-thirty."

So we had macaroni with cheese, beef with broccoli, and noodles with sesame sauce. And fortune cookies with chocolate pudding for dessert. As I was transferring the Chinese leftovers from the cartons into bowls and Dad was feeding Myrtle a piece of beef, he asked, "So. How's your new roommate working out?"

"Roommate? What roommate?"

"You know—George what's-his-name."

"Oh. George." What was I supposed to say? I tried, "He's all right."

Dad went to the sink and turned on the water to wash the dishes. He looked disappointed. Was he jealous that George was living with Mom and me?

"But I really don't like him," I added. I looked around Dad's neat, efficient apartment. "You wouldn't believe how sloppy he is. Dirty shoes and socks everywhere, and he has creepy taste in music."

We laughed about what a slob George was, and I changed the subject by asking Dad if I could go to Sue's to sleep over on Saturday night.

* * *

Our second week with Mr. J. wasn't any better than the first. Work, work, work. On Thursday we had to show him our regulation gym clothes. Our first gym class of the year was on Friday and everyone *had* to be prepared.

"Gym suit inspection, class," Mr. J. announced during homeroom. "Put your uniforms on your desks. Sneakers and socks to the left. Gray T-shirt in the top right corner. Under the shirt the navy cotton shorts. Neatly folded, please."

Bags rustled as we unpacked our clothes. When the room was quiet again and we were all at attention, Mr. J. walked up and down the aisles, his hands behind his back, for the inspection.

When he got to Rita's desk he picked up her shorts. "*Miss* Trono, what fabric would you say this is?"

"Nylon, Mr. Jackson." Rita wasn't even blushing or trembling. "They're running shorts."

"And what kind of shorts are you supposed to have, Miss Trono?"

She looked him right in the eye. "Cotton, Mr. Jackson. I'll have them tomorrow."

"Good."

Mr. J. strode up our aisle. By the time he got to my desk my hands were all sweaty with nervousness. I checked my desk one more time. Everything was in order. I glanced over at Josh's desk. Shorts, shirt, no sneakers.

Mr. J. stood between our desks. I sat up a little straighter. "Fine, Miss Granger," he said as he turned to Josh. Mr. J.'s hands were still behind his back—at my eye level. They looked as big as Myrtle.

"Where are your sneakers, Mr. Greene?" he asked.

Josh pulled a foot from under his desk and raised it

toward Mr. J. "My sneakers are on my feet, Mr. Jackson. They're the only pair of shoes I got."

I thought Mr. J. would be real mad and mean about that because he said we were supposed to have sneakers to leave in school just for gym. But he wasn't. He didn't say anything about the shoes and picked up Josh's T-shirt. As it unfolded the words "Sing Sing Penitentiary" formed out of the folds. It looked like any other shirt when it was folded, so how'd Mr. J. know that out of the thirty-one gray T-shirts in our room that was the one to check?

Everyone but Josh *laughed*. We couldn't help it. We'd been so good for two whole weeks. It wasn't the way we used to laugh with big rolls of deep ha-ha's. It was nervous—a little like the scaredy-cat wimps we were becoming.

Josh looked Mr. J. right in the eye and said, "I'll wear it inside out, Mr. Jackson, sir." Mr. J. folded the shirt back up and handed it to Josh. "See me after school, Mr. Greene, sir."

The next day we were all lined up in the gym in the same rows as in our classroom, waiting for Mr. J. to come out of the locker room. Rita had on cotton shorts, and Josh had on a new gray T-shirt and the same old sneakers.

The swinging doors of the gym pushed open. A beautiful, black muscle machine that had been hiding in Mr. J.'s suits took giant strides across the old wooden floor of the gym. Josh let out a breath of appreciation and mumbled to me, "That's incredible."

Mr. J.—in blue shorts, gray T-shirt, new sneakers, and ten thousand muscles—stood in front of us with his hands on his hips. "Ladies and gentlemen," he said without raising his voice the way gym teachers usually do. "We'll begin with twenty minutes of calisthenics. To start, four sets of jumping jacks. Follow me. Out-in. Out-in. One-two. One-two. Out-in. Out-in."

As he jumped with us I watched his muscles ripple in the bands of afternoon sun. We creaked and stomped as we moved. He barely touched the ground. By the fourth set I stopped admiring Mr. J.'s body and worried about breathing. Sit-ups, knee bends, leg lifts, more jumping jacks, and lots of sweat. You'd think we were training for the Olympics.

Mr. Jackson encouraged us to keep going. "That's the way. Don't stop now. Just give me three more of those push-ups. One. Two. Three. Good."

I finally figured out what made Mr. J. happy—torturing innocent children.

After we jogged around the gym ten times Mr. J. said we'd spend the last fifteen minutes of the class throwing baskets—now that we were warmed up! As we lined up I pulled my sweaty T-shirt away from my stomach and tried to slow down my breathing. Josh's breathing was already even. He was skinny but strong. He'd also been the best basketball shot in the sixth grade. I was second-best. Which is why at summer camp I took basketball three sports periods out of three.

One after another we took our turns at the foul line. Poor Rita missed three out of her three tries and slumped off toward the back of the line. Mr. J. made a mark next to her name in his rollbook. No one had ever kept track of our baskets before. Then he called her back and showed her another way to hold the ball. After two more tries she sank her first basket ever, and Mr. J. noted it next to her name.

When it was Josh's turn, he took his stance with his firm, skinny legs apart, carefully appraised the hoop and swished in two out of three. Mr. J. had him move around the court as he fed him four more. Josh sank two out of the four. Josh looked good. He must have been practicing during the summer, too. I hadn't planned on that. Mr. J. smiled—sort of—for the first time all year.

As Josh threw me the ball he mouthed the challenge—"Top that." And I did. Swish. Swish. Swish. Three in a row. I moved around as Mr. J. threw me four more. I sank three out of four. Clean. "Very good, Miss Granger," he observed as he made the little marks in his book.

"Just luck," Josh mumbled as I got back in line.

The bell rang. We started off the court.

"Ladies and gentlemen—" (We did it before he finished the sentence.)—"freeze. I'm going to teach everyone to shoot like that. Do you understand?"

"Yes, Mr. Jackson," we answered in unison.

"Miss Trono and Miss Sanders, be prepared to stay after school for half an hour of athletic tutoring next Wednesday. Mr. Cioffi and Mr. Lavigne will stay on Friday. Good afternoon, class."

"Good afternoon, Mr. Jackson."

"He must work out ten thousand hours a week," I commented as I unfolded my sleeping bag.

"I've never seen a *live* person with muscles that *big*," Sue said as she passed Janet the last pizza box with the last slice of pizza.

Janet added, "You've seen a *dead* person with muscles like that?"

"No, silly. I mean *live* instead of a picture in a magazine or something."

Rita, Janet, Louise, and I were sleeping over at

Sue's. I slowly let myself down to my sleeping bag. Every molecule in my body was crying out in pain.

"Oh . . ." Sue groaned as she bent over to unzip her sleeping bag. "He should be arrested for child abuse!"

"I can't even raise my arms they hurt so much," Rita said as she rolled a clump of Louise's red hair in a hot roller to match the hairstyle diagram in the *Teen* magazine that Louise held out for her.

"My mom said it'll be easier next week," Janet said. "And that it's good for 'developing our figures.' "

We all looked at Janet with her tiny waist and already developed chest. "You don't need to worry, my dear," Rita said in her catty adult voice.

Janet gave it back to her, as usual. "But *you* do, my dear. I said it for your benefit."

I hate it when they talk like that, so I said something quick to change the subject. "Do you think Josh Greene can get through the year without talking back to Mr. J. and being turned into mush?"

"I bet you anything he doesn't make it to Thanksgiving," Louise commented as she felt where Rita had put the curlers and checked it against the diagram. She looked up at Rita as she pointed to the diagram. "There are five across the top here. You only put in four."

Rita patted her on the shoulder. "You have thin hair. It will work. Trust me."

I looked at myself in Sue's compact mirror. I had trusted Rita an hour before and now I looked like Shirley Temple. I wrapped one of the bouncy curls around my fingers.

"Is Josh still walking your dog?" Janet asked.

I pictured Josh and Mop rolling around on the floor and felt a jealous rumble in the pit of my stomach.

"Yeah. And he expects *me* to take care of his dumb turtle." I told them about Myrtle and how Josh introduced Myrtle and Mop and how funny it was that Mop always had to know where Myrtle was. But they weren't interested in Myrtle and Mop.

"Josh and Aviva," Janet announced. "The first real romance in our class."

"Yeah," Rita added as she started to unwrap Louise's curls. "You two look great together. Both nice and tall."

"What do you mean—together? I hate his guts." I looked around at them. They were all looking at me with these silly smiles. "I hate Josh Greene. You all know that."

"Sure you do," Louise said. "By the way, you should wear your hair like that to school on Monday. It's a nice feminine touch after you showed him up in gym."

"You've got to watch that, Aviva," Rita warned. "It's okay to do some stuff better than the guys. But not your boyfriend."

I jumped up. "He's not my boyfriend. You're all crazy." I was practically screaming. "I can't stand Josh Greene. He's a jerk. Tell them, Sue."

Sue rolled her eyes upward. "She really hates him." But she didn't sound so convinced herself.

"How could anybody like Josh Greene?" I asked.

"Seems to me, you already do," were Rita's last words on the subject.

My last word on the subject was, "Never!"

CHAPTER FOUR

SEPTEMBER						OCTOBER
Dad S 25	Mom M 26	Mom T 27	Mom W 28	Mom Th 29	Mom F 30	Mom S 1

LOVING, SLOPPY KISSES. THAT'S WHAT MOP GAVE ME WHEN I got back to Mom's after school on Monday. I hadn't seen my dog in a whole week. He looked wonderfully fluffy and clean. Had Josh been brushing him?

"I love you, Mop. You're terrific," I told him as he padded beside me toward my bedroom. I stopped in the doorway and looked around. You didn't have to be Nancy Drew to know *someone* had been staying in my room while I was at my dad's. First of all, it smelled funny. Sort of chemical. Next, there was a cigarette butt on my bureau. Then I noticed my waste-paper basket was full. I'd left it empty. I looked through it for more evidence and found it—an empty nail polish remover bottle and tissues stained with bright red nail polish. Maybe Mom and George had a fight and Mom stayed in here, I thought. But my mother quit smoking years ago and she'd never wear red nail polish.

I opened the window to let out the dead smoke smell and went back to the basket. Toward the bottom, in an empty tissue box I found the torn pieces of a letter. I laid all the pieces on my desk and put them together like a jigsaw puzzle.

33

Dear Mom,

I can't believe what Daddy's gone and done now. Did he tell you? He gave up his apartment with my bedroom and moved in with his creepy girlfriend. Now if I want to come to Burlington to see him I have to stay in her kid's room with a dog that snores. They act so lovey dovey you'd think they were twenty years old. It's disgusting. I hate it here. I wish you hadn't moved to California.

Love,
Cindy

George's daughter, Cindy! And calling my mother a creep! Who'd she think she was? I didn't say she could use my room. Nobody even asked me. I opened the window wider to get all the bad Cindy air out, too. Then I went to the kitchen and called my mom at her office to say I was home from school but that I wasn't okay at all and what business did Cindy have staying in my room. "Wait until you see all the awful things she wrote to her mother about you, Mom. She's horrible."

34

But my mom wasn't interested in the letter or mad at all. "Cindy's a nice young woman, Aviva. I think you two will like each other. Remember, this is a big change in her life, too. We all have to be patient and give her time to adjust."

Time to adjust? Well, she could go adjust in someone else's bedroom!

That's when I decided I wouldn't stand for George O'Connell living in my house. I vowed not to say one unnecessary word to him for as long as I lived. I'd pretend he wasn't there.

That night at dinner, after my mom had left for her computer class and George and I were still eating George's apple pie, I clammed up.

"Love this pie," George said. "If I do say so myself."

I didn't say anything.

"How's basketball going?" he asked.

I didn't answer.

"I understand from your mom that you and Josh have a little competition going there. Well, may the best man . . . or girl . . . win."

I wanted to say, "If you say 'man' you should say 'woman,' not 'girl.' " But I didn't say anything. And I left half of my pie uneaten. If it weren't for dumb old George, I thought, I could've watched television while I ate my dessert.

George pushed his chair back and stood up. "You seem a little down in the dumps tonight. Come on. I'll help you with the dishes."

I got up, scraped the rest of my pie into the garbage, and we cleared the table together. But I didn't say one word the whole time. I could tell I was getting on his nerves because when we were about halfway done with

35

the dishes—him washing, me wiping—he stopped talking too.

The last dish he washed was the platter the meat-loaf had been on. The platter he'd told us, "My grand-mother O'Connell hand painted, little rose after little rose." As I took it from him it slipped right out of my dish towel and fell on the floor. It shattered into ten thousand pieces.

George shouted, "Oh no! Aviva, how could you?" He was so mad I knew he wanted to hit me or something.

But I didn't do it on purpose. It just happened. "I'm sorry," I said.

"No you're not," he said as he squatted on the floor and looked at all those little pieces. "You're not sorry at all."

He was right. I wasn't sorry—not really. I bent down to help pick up the mess. He was holding two halves of a rose, trying to fit the pieces together. "Can you fix it?" I asked.

He looked up at me. He wasn't angry anymore—just real sad. "No, I can't fix it. Listen, why don't you go to your room and do your homework or something. I'll finish in here."

Now he didn't want to be with me.

Mop and I went to my room. I felt like a real creep.

Nothing much happened in school that week except that Josh Greene started spending lunch hours alone in the gym—shooting baskets. Mr. J. said anyone who wanted could practice during lunch hour, but no one else did. Least of all me. How could I after what my friends were saying about us? So Josh got to practice between gym classes and I didn't. It just wasn't fair. But seventh grade was teaching me that not much in life was fair.

"How about 'A Hundred Bottles of Beer on the Wall'? You know that one, Aviva?" George caught my eye in the rearview mirror. We'd been riding in the car for three whole hours and were getting pretty bored.

"Sure," I said as I turned sideways and rested my head on Mop's back. "I know it." Anything to make the weekend go by faster. We were on our way to George's summer cottage. I'd never been there, but I was sure Mom had—lots—while I was at sleep-away camp. We were down to forty-eight bottles of beer when we drove out of the woods and up to the back of a small log cabin—like the kind Abraham Lincoln probably grew up in.

Mop started barking his yippiest, happiest bark and scratched on the window to get out. "Boy oh boy," George said as he opened the door for Mop. "Here we are."

Mop had been there before, too. No doubt about it. He bounded out of the car and was running and jumping and sniffing for squirrels all at the same time.

Mom got out of the car, took a deep breath, and laughed at the blue clear sky. "I love it here!"

George ran around the yard saying things like, "Look, the mums are blooming." And, "See these droppings. Some pretty big deer have been around."

I followed Mop to the edge of the lake. Maybe it won't be such a bad weekend after all, I thought, as I stood on the dock and looked at the still water dappled with the reflection of the red and gold autumn leaves. It could be fun to come here in the summer—if Mom and George stayed together—and maybe bring Sue.

We went inside. "So," George said as he stretched his arms out. "This is the living/dining room/kitchen." It was the coziest room I'd ever been in. The walls were pine. There was a big stone fireplace, a nice old-fashioned braided rug, a big overstuffed couch, and an old round table. Not a dab of puke green in the whole place.

"Our room is over there." George pointed to a door on the far side of the room. "The next door is to the bathroom. And next to it is Cin . . . is your room." He picked up my little suitcase and headed toward an old pine door with a hand-painted sign warning, "Private. Keep Out."

I stood there looking at the red letters as George opened the door and went in. He turned to me. "Don't pay any attention to that. She made that sign years ago. Cindy's a grown woman now. She's in college."

Some grown-up, I thought, remembering the letter she'd written her mother. I sat on the bed and looked around. It was a little too feminine for me. Sue would have loved it. Wallpaper with tiny blue flowers, a dressing table with a matching fabric skirt, and a white ruffled bedspread. It wasn't exactly my style, but it was fun for a change. Who cared if it was Cindy's room? I'd spend most of my time outside anyway.

I started by walking with Mop around the whole lake—about six miles.

That night we had hamburgers and hot dogs and sat by the fire in the living room. No one said very much. Mom and George were watching the fire like it was a TV set, so I went back to Cindy's Private-Keep-Out room.

When I got under the quilt and put my head on her ruffled pillowcase I wondered if she was sad when *her* parents got divorced. She'd had the rug pulled out from under her too—even if it was puke green. I thought of the mean letter she had written her mother about my mother and remembered all the mean things I had said to my father about her father. I figured she didn't like divorce anymore than I did.

I would never tell my dad this, but here is one great thing about George—besides his summer house. He's a terrific cook. The next morning, on my second helping of blueberry pancakes, I asked him, "Does Cindy come here anymore?"

George grinned at me. I guess because I mentioned Cindy. "Sure she does. In fact she's coming with your mom and me next weekend. She's bringing a friend." Well, I thought. At least she won't be staying in *my* room next weekend. He turned back to the stove to cook some more pancakes for himself. "You should bring a friend the next time we come out," he said over his shoulder. "Josh maybe."

Josh again! "Josh isn't my friend," I told him. "He works for me. I wish everyone would get it out of their heads that we're friends."

My mom was smirking through her blueberry-stained teeth.

"It's not a joke, *Mother*," I told her. "It happens to be the truth. Josh Greene may be your friend, but he's my employee."

"Of course," she said. But she was still grinning. "You can bring Sue."

"Good," I said. "That's just what I intend to do."

I put my feet up on Mop and bent under the table to give him a piece of pancake from my hand.

Before we left on Sunday afternoon I made the bed and checked that I hadn't left anything in the wastepa-

39

per basket. Then I sat down at the dainty dressing table and wrote on a piece of school paper.

Dear Cindy,

    Thank you for the use of your room. It is very pretty.

        Sincerely Yours,

        Aviva Granger

Maybe that would teach her some manners.

CHAPTER FIVE

Mom	Dad	Dad	Dad	Dad	Dad	Dad
S 2	M 3	T 4	W 5	Th 6	F 7	S 8

MONDAY NIGHT IT WAS BACK TO MY BEDROOM AT DAD'S. Every night a different bed—Saturday at George's, Sunday at Mom's, and Monday at Dad's. I was tired of packing and unpacking and felt sort of sick to my stomach when I got into bed. Myrtle was asleep under my nightstand. "You know Myrtle," I whispered. "I'm a little bit like you. I have to carry my house around with me, too. Only mine's in my suitcase and yours is on your back." I moved around trying to find a more comfortable position.

Though I don't remember doing it, I must have fallen asleep because later, in the middle of the night, I woke up. My pajamas were wet. Had I wet the bed? My life had been upsetting, but this was ridiculous. I turned on the light and threw off the covers. Blood. On my pajamas. It took me about two seconds to realize that I'd gotten my first period.

Mom and I had figured it would come when I was at summer camp, so I had sanitary napkins hidden in an extra pillowcase at the bottom of my trunk. But it didn't come at camp and I got sick of wondering when it would and had forgotten all about it. Now here it was when I least expected it. At Dad's. He certainly wouldn't have any sanitary napkins. No way was I going to tell him. What would I say? "Daddy, dear, I just got my period for the first time. Would you mind getting up and going out to the all-night pharmacy and buying me some sanitary napkins?''

After I washed my p.j. bottoms I went into the kitchen and unrolled some paper towels, folded them into a packet, and pinned it to a pair of underpants.

I got back into bed, lay on my back, and rested my hands on my stomach. Maybe I'd get cramps, like Mom said she did when she was a teenager. But then I wasn't a teenager yet, so maybe I wouldn't. I turned over on my stomach. Maybe I wouldn't be able to go to sleep for the rest of the night, but just lie there wondering what if I bleed all over my clothes in school tomorrow? And, how will I get sanitary napkins? And, how much blood will there be? And, how long will it last? I wished I could remember more of what my mom said during our little talk before I went to camp.

As I was counting the girls I knew who already had ''it,'' I fell asleep.

''Rise and shine,'' Dad said in a not very shiny voice as he rapped on my bedroom door the next morning. When I finally got myself put together to go to school, I felt like I had a roll of paper towels between my legs. I practically did. Could you tell? I turned around in front of the full-length mirror to look at my bottom half this way and that. I checked out okay.

But by the middle of Social Studies I was pretty uncomfortable. That's when I remembered the vending machine in the girls' room. I raised my hand. ''Please, Mr. Jackson, may I be excused.'' Everyone turned and looked at me. No one had asked to leave the room before. That's how afraid we were of Mr. J. My hands were clammy with nervousness as I dropped them back in my lap.

Mr. Jackson said, "Yes, Miss Granger. You may."

This is how the sanitary napkin vending machine in the third floor girls' restroom at St. Agnes works. Not at all. This is what the paper towels in the third floor girls' restroom at St. Agnes School are like. Thin and scratchy.

I was pretty miserable when I came out of the girls' room into the hall. Maybe I should go to my mom's at lunchtime and call her at work, I thought. But then what if George were there? What excuse could I give for going home during a D-A-D week?

I heard a rustle of skirt and clinking of rosary beads. Sister Bernard Marie was rushing to her classroom with a hot-off-the-press mimeographed test. She stopped short in front of me. Her blue eyes sparkled at mine. "Good gracious, child, what's wrong?"

Tears collected in my eyes. I was speechless. I looked at the floor.

"Oh my," she said. "Is it that time of the month?" Sister Bernard Marie could read minds, too. The difference was she used it when it was important!

I nodded my head and pointed at the door marked "Girls." "The machine's broken." I mumbled.

"Oh, I see." She glanced toward the open door of her classroom where thirty nervous and noisy sixth graders were waiting for their test. She checked her watch. "Listen, Aviva dear, lunch break is in thirty minutes. Can you manage until then?"

I nodded.

She sighed. "Good. Why don't you bring your lunch over to the convent and we'll take care of this little problem." She patted me on the arm. "All right?"

I nodded again. "Thank you, Sister."

I watched her veil and floor-length black skirt billow

43

behind her as she rushed down the corridor to settle her class down.

Sister Bernard Marie was all cheery and glad to see me when she opened the convent door—like I was special company. I'd never been in the convent before. Actually, it looked like anybody else's house, only cleaner and quieter.

"Now," she said. "Let's take care of first things first. The bathroom is the second door on your right." She pointed down the hall. "You'll find a box of pads in the cabinet under the sink. Just pull off the paper strip and stick it to your panties."

When I came out she was carrying a tray with a chicken sandwich, a salad, a pot of tea, and two cups. "I thought we'd eat on the picnic table in the backyard," she said. "Enjoy this beautiful Indian summer day."

I was much more comfortable as I followed her through the kitchen into the backyard. We pulled the picnic table over to a sunny spot and put out our lunches.

Sister looked at my soggy peanut butter and jelly sandwich. "Why don't we share our lunches?" she asked.

"It's okay. I'm not all that hungry today."

She didn't pay any attention to what I said and took half of my sandwich and gave me half of her absolutely delicious chicken sandwich. I was glad that I had a brownie I could split with her to make up a bit for the sloppy sandwich I had thrown together.

"Is this the first time, dear?" she asked as she swallowed her last bite of sticky peanut butter.

"Uh-huh." I nodded.

"Did you tell your mother?"

44

"I'm at my dad's this week."

She nodded. "Oh, yes, that joint custody business. Well then, it's up to me." She stood up and rustled off, her veil flying, her beads rattling. She was back in a jiffy with a giant-size box of sanitary napkins in a used A&P shopping bag. Did nuns get their periods? It sure looked like it.

I just stared at it. What was I going to do with that bag *all afternoon?* "Thank you," I said.

"Maybe I should bring this to my classroom," Sister said. "And you can pick it up after school. Now let's have some tea to toast you into womanhood."

She beamed as we clinked cups. "Welcome, my dear. Welcome."

After school I washed Sister's boards and watered her plants while she helped some kid who couldn't understand how to carry in fractions. After about half an hour I figured everyone had cleared out of the school-yard, and I could go to the bus stop without ten thousand people asking me what was in the shopping bag.

I decided having your period probably isn't so bad if you're not worried about other people knowing.

When I stepped through the big metal door all I could see was a bunch of little kids fighting over whose turn was next on the swings.

I turned the corner of the building to come face to face with Cioffi. "Hey, Josh. Here she is." I figured if I ran I was just asking for trouble. I decided to stay calm and act natural.

"Hi, birdbrain," I said to Cioffi. "Didn't know you liked school so much." And to Josh, "Don't you have a dog to walk?"

"I'm on my way," Josh answered. "But first I want

to know what you were doing at the convent during lunch . . ." He stared at the shopping bag. ". . . And what you've got in that bag."

Forget calm. Forget natural. I broke into a run with my book bag flapping on my shoulder and the shopping bag of *sanitary napkins* flapping against my leg. Of course Josh and Cioffi weren't loaded down with anything as tacky or heavy as school books. Otherwise, they wouldn't have caught me.

Josh held me from behind by the elbows while Cioffi wrenched the bag from my hand. They thought it was a great joke, but I was fighting back tears.

"Still Sister Bernard Marie's pet?" Josh teased.

Cioffi looked in the bag and laughed hysterically. Josh turned around without letting go of me as Cioffi held the bag open for him to look for himself. I was kicking and screaming. "Let me go, you . . . you—"

"Look what she's got." Cioffi was laughing. "Some present!"

Josh let go of me.

I was beet red from embarrassment, but my color couldn't come close to the shade of red that flushed Josh Greene's face when he saw the box of sanitary napkins.

"You jerk, Cioffi." He hit Cioffi on the arm. "That's not funny."

"Ow!" Cioffi grabbed his arm where Josh had walloped him. But he just wouldn't give up. "Didn't ya see what it was?"

Josh didn't bother to answer him, but ran through the schoolyard in the direction of Elm Street where Mop was waiting to go for his afterschool walk.

Now I was as angry as I was embarrassed. "Why don't you grow up, Cioffi," I yelled as I hit him on his other arm. I'm at least six inches taller than Cioffi and

46

twice as strong. I had to resist the temptation to wallop him good. Anyway my bus was coming.

I thought of just leaving the bag there. But what if Sister saw it? Besides, I needed what was in it. I grabbed the bag and ran to catch the bus to my dad's. "These are for my mother, you know," I yelled back to Cioffi.

CHAPTER SIX

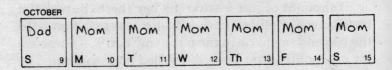

MY FIRST PERIOD HAD COME AND GONE AND THE ONLY PER-son who knew about it (for sure) was Sister Bernard Ma-rie. I decided to wait until I got back to my mom's to tell her.

Monday night my mother got home from work be-fore George. He had a meeting and wasn't even coming home for supper. Mom was in a tizzy trying to figure out how to do all the housework she hadn't done on the weekend because she was at George's cabin. There were clothes to wash, the kitchen floor to clean, the rugs to vacuum. All the stuff she usually does on Saturday morning. Then there was supper to cook.

I was helping her with the wash by separating the colored clothes from the white ones. George had even more dirty socks than he had old shoes. As soon as I threw one in the colored pile Mop would grab it in his mouth and shake it. Some dogs don't have very dis-criminating taste. I'd brought my dirty clothes from Dad's and was adding them to the pile. As I threw my pajamas onto the white/light pile I said, "Guess what happened to me last week?"

Mom mumbled, "Maybe we could have macaroni and cheese," before she looked up at me to ask, "What? What happened to you?"

I tossed my navy blue sweatshirt in with the colored clothes. "I got my period."

48

"That's ni—" She dropped George's jeans and turned toward me. "You what?"

I said it louder as I threw my gym socks in with the whites. "I got my period." Before I knew what happened I was inside a big hug.

"Oh, my baby," my mom said into my hair. She kissed me on the head, on the forehead, and on both cheeks.

"My little girl." She was crying. I have a very sentimental mother. She held me at arm's length and looked me over. "Are you all right?"

I shrugged my shoulders. "Of course I'm all right. It happens to everyone. Except guys. Even nuns."

"But why didn't you or your father tell me?"

I couldn't believe her. "Mom, I wouldn't tell *Dad*."

"Well," she said smiling. "This most definitely calls for a celebration! Forget the wash. Forget the floor. And most of all, forget the macaroni and cheese. We'll go out to eat. Two *women* out on the town."

And we did. Just Mom and me.

I never really liked Geography very much before Mr. J. taught us. I had liked school a lot better before Mr. J., but not Geography. He had a neat way of describing places that made you feel like you were right there. On Wednesday he began like this, "Now class, close your eyes. You are in Brazil at the equator. Your body is sweating under a noon sun that is hot and strong. You squint your eyes against the glare as you dip your canoe paddle into the murky green water of the Amazon—"

We were all dodging crocodiles, swatting mosquitoes, and waiting for a torrential rain to cool us off when Mr. J. interrupted himself. "Well, Miss Saunders. You seem to have missed the boat. Would you kindly bring the note you took from Miss Trono up to me."

One by one we'd opened our eyes to watch Janet bring the note to Mr. J. The first note of the year. When Sister Bernard Marie caught you passing a note, she tore it up without reading it. Then you had to stay after school and write a letter to each of the three TV networks telling them which of their shows you thought was the dumbest and why. Before the letters went out you had to read them out loud to the whole class during homeroom.

What would Mr. J. do?

"What do we have here?" he asked as he opened the note and began to read it out loud. How embarrassing for Rita, I thought.

"Janet," it began. "No doubt about it. It's true love. Aviva and Josh. Have you noticed how he's always looking at her."

I could have died. Or killed.

"He's not looking at *me*," I yelled out. "He's copying my work."

At the same time Josh screeched, "Aviva? You think I got taste in my feet?"

Everyone laughed except me, Josh . . . and Mr. J.

In two seconds the class was dead silent. Mr. J. forgot all about our canoe trip and made us do the questions in our geography book on the Amazon—all the way through recess. At least Josh Greene did his own work for a change.

Maybe I wouldn't invite Janet and Rita to my Halloween birthday party this year.

The big disadvantage of being in the back of the room is that you're the last one to leave. Everyone said, "Good afternoon, Mr. Jackson," as they passed him standing next to the doorway at his Marine sergeant straightest. I didn't. I needed all my strength to keep from stomping on his feet as my sneakers passed his shiny black shoes.

Once we were outdoors Rita came at me from one side and Janet from the other. "Aviva," they said in unison. "I'm sorry." I gave them each a good shove and ran all the way home.

Mop knew I was upset even before I got the door all the way open. Instead of big jumps and slurpy kisses I got soft whimpers and wet little kisses on my fingers.

"I don't believe it!" I yelled to Mop as I slammed the door. "How could Mr. Jackson be so *mean*? How could Rita be so *dumb*?" We automatically went into the kitchen, but I was too mad to eat. I left a message with the receptionist at my mom's office to tell her I was home and took Mop for a quick walk. Then I lay on the couch and plotted my revenge. For Mr. J., a whole month without *any* exercise and a diet of *only* sweets, fatty foods, and sodas. Let him watch his muscles turn to blubber. Janet wouldn't be allowed to take a bath or wash her hair for the entire month. And Rita would have tape over her mouth so she couldn't talk. Maybe the punishments should last for a year, I thought, as I studied the crack in the ceiling and rubbed behind Mop's ears. Thinking up the punishments didn't make me feel any better.

I turned on my soap opera. Jason was blaming his partner L.B. for taking shortcuts that caused the pollution that gave his mother the lung disease. L.B. told Eleanor that if Jason didn't leave him alone he was going to tell him the truth about the affair that they (Eleanor and L.B.) were having.

I didn't feel a smidgen of pity for Eleanor or Jason or L.B. They didn't have to go to school tomorrow and face a whole class of kids who'd heard, "It's true love. Aviva and Josh." And believed it.

Maybe I should write Mr. J. a note myself, I thought. At least I'd be doing something real. I sat at my desk and tried to think of what to say. The first three tries could have gotten me thrown out of school. Like, "Mr. J. you're a mean creep." Stuff like that.

Finally I was satisfied that I had a note I would have the courage to leave on Mr. J.'s desk.

Dear Mr. Jackson,
    You should consider the feelings of innocent people when you read notes to the class.
                    Sincerely Yours,
                    Aviva Granger

P.S.
Please don't read this note out loud to the class.
    Thank you.
    A.G.

The next day Josh was absent, for which I was very grateful. The day was quiet, normal, and boring.

I kept the note for Mr. J. in my desk. After the final bell he took his position at the door. Since I was the last one out I could drop the note on his desk without anyone noticing. Which is what I did.

As I passed by Mr. J. I looked him straight in the eye and said, "Good afternoon, Mr. Jackson."

Friday was gym. I prayed that Josh would be absent again. But there he was in a corner of the classroom dribbling an imaginary ball and trying out a move that Mr. J. was showing him. In the last gym class Josh had been better at shooting baskets than I was. I thought Mr. J. was giving me harder shots. Rita thought I missed a couple of baskets on purpose and congratulated me on "good strategy."

"Today we'll cut the calisthenics short," Mr. J. announced when we were all lined up in our gym outfits. We wisely resisted the temptation to cheer. "After we've warmed up we'll break into two groups for a basketball game." He made Josh captain of one team and me captain of the other. Both teams had a mix of boys and girls. We all played pretty good, better than Mr. J. thought we would.

Rita was on my team. She didn't want me missing baskets on purpose now. "Come on, Aviva," she yelled. "We can do it. Let's show them who's tops." And we did. I sunk the last basket and we won by one point.

"Good, class. Very good," Mr. J. said after the bell rang and we were in our frozen basketball positions. "Soon you'll be ready to take on the eighth grade."

"It's so romantic," Rita sighed when we were
53

changing out of our gym clothes. "The lovers competed in sports. Now they unite their talents to lead the team to victory."

I slapped her bottom with my T-shirt. "Rita, if you don't cut that stuff out I'm going to use your head for a basketball." I was really getting mad.

"Touchy!" Rita said. "Can't you take a little teasing?"

"No," I hollered.

She knew I meant it.

"A turtle. That's it, Aviva. You should be a turtle." Saturday night Sue was sleeping over at my place. George and Mom had gone to a dinner party so we had the place to ourselves. We were eating popcorn and planning my annual Halloween birthday party. Sue jumped off the couch and paced the puke green rug. "We can cut octagons out of cardboard and put them together with masking tape to get the shape right."

"And paint it with poster paint," I added.

"Right." Sue sat down with a satisfied plop.

"What about my head? How can we make it look slimy?" I asked.

The phone rang. It was Rita and Janet calling from Janet's house. We had a phone-in pajama party. First we put our radios on the same station and got sodas. Then we settled down to talk, Sue on the kitchen phone, me on the one in the living room.

"What are you guys doing?" Rita asked.

"Planning Aviva's party," Sue said. She could see me from her perch on the kitchen stool. I signaled her not to tell them about what I was going to be for Halloween.

"But don't ask what Aviva's going to be," Sue went on.

Rita and Janet were silent. They didn't start guessing the way they always do.

"You don't expect us to wear costumes this year, do you?" Rita asked.

"And trick or treat," Janet added.

Sue said, "We always do."

"Always do doesn't mean always will," Rita said. "We're in junior high this year. We shouldn't be doing that kid stuff anymore. I really don't want to."

"Me either," Janet said.

"I don't think any of your friends do, Aviva."

Janet said, "Come on, Aviva. Let's have a *real* party. You know, maybe invite some of the eighth-grade *boys*."

"Yeah," Rita commented. "You could still have food and presents."

"Only instead of trick or treat, we'll dance and stuff," added Janet.

"I don't know," I said.

"There are some real cute guys in the eighth grade," Sue said. "Rita, if she invited Tim Lewis do you think he'd come?"

"I bet he would," Rita said. "Bob and Sam, too. They hang out with you-know-who."

And they all started gossiping about the eighth-grade boys.

Maybe they're right, I thought. Maybe we're too old for trick or treat.

"So it would be more like an ordinary birthday party," I said.

"Yeah. But we'd still make Halloween decorations," Sue said.

55

"And have lots of candy," Rita said.

"And boys," Janet added.

"Okay," I said.

I was glad I hadn't already made my turtle costume.

Mop came over and put his head on my lap. While Sue and Janet and Rita chattered on about the eighth-grade boys, I scratched behind Mop's ears and wondered whether I would invite Josh you-know-who Greene to my party this year.

Mop looked up at me with his wonderful, sweet sad-eyed dog look.

CHAPTER SEVEN

OCTOBER

Mom	Dad	Dad	Dad	Dad	Dad	Dad
S 16	M 17	T 18	W 19	Th 20	F 21	S 22

THE BIGGEST DIFFERENCE FOR ME IN GOING BACK TO DAD'S every other week was not being greeted by Mop when I got in from school. No welcoming barks and yelps. No fluffing up his fur and saying, "How you doing you great, furry lug?" Or, "That's my sweet dog."

At Dad's I was greeted by Myrtle. This is how a turtle says hello. Very quietly. This is how a turtle jumps up and kisses you. Not at all.

"Hi, Myrt," I yelled when I came in on Thursday. Then the search began. Where was Myrtle? Some days she'd be in her big pan and sleeping under water. But the night before I'd put her on the floor, so she could be anyplace.

The only times I'm glad Dad's apartment is so small is when I'm vacuuming and when I'm looking for Myrtle.

"Myrtle?" I called over and over as I looked under Dad's bed.

No Myrtle.

One thing you don't have to worry about when you're looking for a turtle is that it'll go quick and hide someplace else. Now I wasn't looking for Myrtle because I was afraid she'd starve to death or anything. Turtles can go for months and months without eating. I wanted to say hello and know where she was, so I wouldn't just bump into her, or worse, step on her.

57

I looked under my bed.

No Myrtle.

But I did find my other rainbow-striped sock. I'd been looking for it the whole week before—at Mom's. At least now I knew where it was.

How about the kitchen? Maybe Myrtle was under the refrigerator. She wasn't. The cabinet door under the counter was open. "You in there, Myrtle?" I asked as I moved the boxes of cereal and crackers around.

No Myrtle.

But there was a box of Shredded Wheat. I took it out and looked at it. Half empty. Pretty weird, considering that Dad and I hate Shredded Wheat so much that we call it shredded cardboard. I put it back and closed the cabinet.

I went into the living room to continue my search for Myrtle. I got on my hands and knees and put my cheek on the floor to look under the couch. Something glittered in the dark.

Myrtle?

I brushed my hand along the floor. It rubbed over a small, hard object.

Not Myrtle.

I picked it up, pulled out my hand, and sat back on the rug.

A rhinestone earring.

Whose?

It certainly wasn't mine.

I put the earring in my pocket and went to search the bathroom for Myrtle. Was she hiding between the shower curtain and the bathtub? Something was there. I pulled the shower curtain away.

Not Myrtle.

I picked up a half-empty plastic bottle of avocado

cream rinse. It wasn't mine. And Dad would never use phony stuff like that. He was into your basic No Brand shampoo.

So Dad has a girlfriend I thought as I went into the hall to put her cream rinse in the closet with our other drugstore-type stuff.

"Hss—ss." I jumped at the sound of Myrtle pulling in her head and flippers under her shell. The sound came from the pile of dirty sheets on the floor. Myrtle.

I patted her on the shell. "Hey, Myrt, it's just me." She poked out her dark freckled head and stared at me. Then out came the flippers. Myrtle was ready to follow me. As I stood up I came eye level with two boxes of sanitary napkins. I guessed my mom had told my dad. Well, at least no one was expecting me to buy them.

As I put a box under each arm and turned to go to my room, a thousand light bulbs went off in my head. What a great idea! Just behind the boxes of sanitary napkins I'd spotted the Ace bandage Dad used last year when he sprained his ankle. The idea was, what if tomorrow I have a "sprained ankle" and can't go to gym? Then maybe everyone would shut up about Josh and me. After I put the boxes in my closet I came back for Myrtle and the Ace bandage.

"So pumpkin," Dad said about halfway through his meat loaf that night. "How's your mother's boyfriend doing?"

I put more ketchup on my meat loaf. "I don't know. All right, I guess." I always got the feeling that when Dad asked me about George he wanted me to say something mean or funny. He certainly didn't want me to tell him how well Mom and George got along or that George was a good cook or anything like that. Dad's asking the question reminded me of a question I had for him.

"You're always asking me about Mom's boyfriend. What about your girlfriend?"

Dad put ketchup on his meat loaf. It was a little dry. "Girlfriend? Why you're my girl," he said.

"Yeah," I said. "But I don't use the avocado cream rinse that I found in the bathroom. And neither of us eats Shredded Wheat that I found in the kitchen cabinet. And what about this?" I held up the rhinestone earring. "I don't think it would look very good on you."

Dad was beet red with embarrassment. You'd think I was the parent who'd caught his kid at a lie.

"Uh . . ." He hesitated.

"So who is she? Or who are they?"

"Who?" he said, stalling.

"Your girlfriends."

"Well, now. You know I have friends who happen to be women, Aviva—my colleagues at the college, other teachers. Sometimes I'll have one of them over, for a business supper. Just friends, not girlfriends."

"You serve them Shredded Wheat and avocado cream rinse for supper? Come on, Dad."

He held up his hand. "All right. You got me. Miriam. Her name's Miriam. I think you'd like her. She's . . ."

He got all enthusiastic and mushy about how great Miriam was and that she was so smart and all this stuff I didn't care about at all.

All I cared about was whether she had kids who'd want to use my bedroom. She didn't.

The next day, after Dad kissed me good-bye at the bus stop, I sat on the curb and took the Ace bandage out

60

of my knapsack. Before the bus got there I wrapped my ankle up tight. Problem was I couldn't tie my sneaker. Finally I just took out the lace.

When I got to school I remembered to limp a little as I walked up the aisle to my seat.

"What happened to you?" Josh blurted out. He'd broken our unspoken agreement not to talk to each other after Rita's lying, stupid, dumb, jerky note.

"Sprained my ankle," I answered without looking at him.

Mr. J. was surprisingly sympathetic, but concerned about the way it was wrapped. "Looks like that bandage isn't going to do you as much good as it should," he said as he looked down at my foot. He sat on his haunches in front of me. "I'd like to do it over for you," he offered.

And he did. First he unwound it. Then he pressed different spots. "Tell me when it hurts," he said.

"Oh, there," I said a couple of times. Could he tell I was faking it?

Actually I was holding back a load of giggles because at the same time he was feeling for the "sprain," his cold fingers were resting on the bottom of the foot. My most ticklish spot of all.

He seemed to believe I'd really hurt it and wrapped it back up again, nice and tight. Then he put a chair in the aisle so I could elevate it.

By then the whole class had come in and were in their seats, mostly turned around to see what Mr. J. was doing to my foot.

"I guess I can't take gym today," I told him after I said "Thank you."

"Certainly not. I only hope that you'll be back on the court for the game against the eighth grade next month.'' He turned to Josh. ''Otherwise it'll all be up to you, Mr. Greene.''

''I can handle it,'' Josh boasted.

Gym's pretty boring when you just sit there with your foot up on the bleacher watching everyone else play basketball. Josh's team slaughtered the rest of the class. He was good—very good. I figured that meant since I was as good as he was, then I was good—very good. Which made me feel stupid for wasting a whole gym period because of some silly gossip.

When I got back to Dad's after school the first thing I did was take off the bandage. My ankle felt funny after being wrapped up tight like that and being limped on all day. Then I found Myrtle—back under the sheets in the linen closet—and settled down to watch my soap opera and wait for Sue to call about what time she could come over on Saturday to go shopping with me for party stuff. We were going to pick out decorations and two new records for dancing.

When the doorbell rang I thought it was on the soap opera. It rang again—our apartment bell. Who could be at the door? Dad had his own key—besides it was too early for him. Friday was his late day. I knew I had to be careful and not let anyone in who said they were the phone company or something. I was feeling nervous when I called through the door, ''Who is it?''

''It's me.''

My mother?

I opened it quickly. She was pale and strange looking.

She came in and closed the door behind her as I asked, ''What is it? What happened?''

"Mop . . . Mop . . ." The tears started streaming down her face. "Oh, baby, Mop got hit by a car."

"No," I screamed. "No."

"And . . . and he's dead."

I felt upside down and inside out and every way but right. I didn't know what to do with the strange feelings that ripped at me. "No," I screamed again. "Mommy, no . . . no . . . no."

She put her arms around me. I pulled away. "Tell me 'No.' "

"I can't," she said. "I just can't. It happened. It's true."

"I don't believe it. I want to see him."

She put her arm around my shoulder. "Come on. We'll go there."

As we went down the elevator I tried to keep it from being real. Maybe the person who had called my mother at work had made a mistake. Maybe it was someone else's sheepdog. Or maybe Mop was just unconscious—like with a concussion. I tried both of these ideas out on my mom when we got in the car.

"We'll see," she said. "I got the call at work from Mrs. Sullivan, the lady in the house right next to the park. She said he was dead."

"How? I don't understand. Didn't you close the door? How'd he get out?"

Mom hesitated before she said, "It was an accident. Josh was walking him. A car was going too fast to stop. It didn't even stop after it hit Mop."

"Josh? He didn't keep Mop on the leash?"

"It's not Josh's fault," was the last thing my mom said until we got to the park.

I slumped in the seat and cried.

63

"I left a message for your father at the college," Mom said as we were getting out of the car.

I could see Josh's back hunched over Mop on the grass by the road. I broke into a run. "Get away!" I shouted. "Get away from my dog." He got up, but couldn't look at me. He was crying, too, but I didn't care.

He just turned and walked away.

I bent down to touch my dog. He was still warm. Maybe I was right about him being unconscious. "Mop," I yelled as I stroked his fur and rubbed behind his ears. "Mop, wake up. I'm right here. You'll see—you're going to be all right. I'll take care of you."

He didn't move. I put my head on his chest. It's hard to get a heartbeat through all that fur, I thought.

My mother bent down beside me. "Aviva, honey, he's dead."

I pushed his closed eyelids open with my thumb. Only white showed. I put my head on Mop's chest and cried, "No. No."

The next thing I knew my dad was there. "Come on, Aviva. Let's take Mop away from here."

We put Mop on our old red and black plaid camping blanket that Dad kept in the trunk of his car and we put him on the backseat. While we were doing it I could see Josh just standing there, leaning against a tree. As soon as Mop was in the car I turned to Josh Greene and yelled out, "Murderer! He's dead. Mop's dead and it's your fault."

"Aviva," my dad yelled. "Stop that. It's not true. Stop it!"

"It's true," I yelled. "And he knows it."

Josh turned and started to walk out of the park.

My mom called out, "Josh, wait." She started after

him. Just then George pulled up in his car. He'd heard me. And he saw Josh.

In an instant he was out of the car. "Stay with Aviva," George yelled to my mom as he ran by us. "I'll take care of Josh." As I got in the backseat with Mop and Mom, and Dad got in the front, I saw George catch up with Josh and put his arm around his shoulder.

"Why don't I drop you and Aviva off," my dad said to my mom as we pulled away from the park. "I'll take care of Mop's . . . body."

I was stroking my sweet dog's fur. "What are you going to do with him?" I asked.

"I'll bury him—in the woods. Don't you think that's the best place? He loved it there, with you."

"I want to help," I said.

My mom turned around to look at me and Mop. "Are you sure?" she asked.

"Yes."

"I want to help, too," she told my dad.

First we went to Mom's to get a shovel, then we drove as far into the woods as we could. When we got Mop out of the car Mom and Dad carried him in the blanket and I walked behind them with the shovel. I told them where I wanted the body to be buried—a clearing in the middle of the pine forest. It's the spot that Mop and I used to go to when the weather was beautiful and we wanted to be in the country.

We all took turns shoveling, but Dad did most of it. All the time I kept looking at Mop, praying he would move, stopping every once in a while to feel for a heartbeat. But minute by minute Mop was getting colder and colder.

No one said very much, except for things like, "What a wonderful dog." And "Such a friendly, sweet

65

dog." And "Remember when he was a puppy, how he used to jump on your lap?" My mom and dad were crying the whole time, too.

When the hole was deep enough, we lowered the blanket with Mop into the hole. Dad wrapped the blanket around him so you couldn't see him anymore.

"You and Mom go back to the car now," Dad said. "I'll finish."

"No," I answered. And I stayed and helped until the hole was filled and Mop covered with earth.

We stood there for a minute, looking at the mound of dirt. "Let's go," my mom said. "It's getting dark."

I didn't want to leave my dog in the dark, in the dirt, dead in the earth. I wanted to crawl into the earth with him. I didn't want to live without my dog.

We dropped Mom off at the house and Dad and I went back to his apartment. I threw myself on the bed, rolled over on my back and thought about my dog.

Seven years—over half my life—I'd spent with Mop. Dead? How could it be?

Dad knocked on my door. "Aviva. The telephone for you."

"I can't," I called back.

"Open the door," he said in his no-nonsense voice.

When I let him in I could see his eyes were still red from crying. "Who is it?" I asked.

"It's your mother's boyfriend. He wants to talk to you."

"I don't want—"

"Aviva," my dad interrupted. "George lived with Mop, too. He's upset. I think you should talk to him."

I sat on the couch and picked up the receiver. "Hello."

"Aviva, it's George."

"I know."

"I'm . . . I'm so sorry about Mop. He was a wonderful dog. It's a terrible loss for you. For all of us."

I could hear tears in George's voice. I got all choked up again. "Thank you," I said. "For calling."

"And Aviva?"

"Yes."

"You know Josh is upset, too."

"He should be. He killed Mop."

"It was an accident. He loved Mop, too."

I jumped up off the couch and shouted into the receiver. "He didn't have Mop on a leash."

"He told me how it happened," George said. "He was playing with Mop when a squirrel—"

"I don't want to hear it," I screamed as I hung up the phone.

My dad was standing there watching me. I glared at him. "It was Josh's fault," I told him.

Then I went back to my room. Later Dad brought me some tea and toast. I guess I fell asleep because the next thing I knew . . .

It was late afternoon and I was alone in the woods looking for Mop. When I came to our special clearing I saw a fresh mound of dirt. I heard a scratching noise in the ground as I walked toward it. It was Mop, scratching and whimpering to get out. He was buried alive! I started clawing the dirt out of the grave with my hands. Trying to get to him. Calling, "Mop, I'm coming. It'll be all right. I'll get you out," over and over. I dug and dug until I was in this big hole. My arms ached. I kept digging. I could still hear him whimpering and scratching. But no matter how deep I dug I couldn't find Mop. Finally I was so tired I started crying and lay down in the hole. I looked up at the sky. It was getting dark.

My parents, each holding a shovel, appeared above me, at the edge of the grave. They were crying, too. They each threw a shovelful of dirt on me.

"Stop," I yelled. More dirt rained on me. "Stop. I'm not dead."

I screamed it, but no sound came out. "Stop, stop."

My dad was shaking me.

"I'm not dead. Stop." I could hear my own voice now.

He put his arm around me. "Of course you're not dead. You just had a scary nightmare."

We went into the living room and I told him what happened in my nightmare. Then we told each other about all the wonderful times we had had with Mop.

CHAPTER EIGHT

Dad	Mom	Mom	Mom	Mom	Mom
S 23	M 24	T 25	W 26	Th 27	F 28

SATURDAY I STAYED IN BED ALL DAY. I HAD A TEMPERATURE and a cough. My dad said I was "sick with grief." I didn't watch junk TV all day like I usually do when I'm sick. But I did sleep a lot. And each time I woke up I'd have to remember all over again—Mop's dead.

Sunday morning my temperature was back to normal. Sue came over and Dad took us to brunch. She said how sorry she was about Mop, but that I shouldn't blame Josh for what happened. I wouldn't talk to her about it. Dad took us to a movie, too. I don't even remember what it was about. Some comedy that wasn't very funny.

Monday morning, before Dad dropped me at the bus stop, he said, "Don't be so hard on Josh, Aviva. I think you're blaming him because you're hurting so much. We all used to let Mop off the leash. It could've happened with any of us."

"Don't give me that psychological stuff," I told him. "You're all protecting Josh."

He shook his head and gave me a good-bye kiss on the forehead. "Just don't do or say anything you'll be sorry for," he said.

I got out of the car and waved good-bye to Dad. I won't say anything to Josh I'll be sorry for, I thought, because I'm not going to school today. As soon as Dad's car was out of sight I started to walk. I walked and walked and walked until I was at the edge of the woods where we had buried Mop.

It was another beautiful Indian summer day. The leaves on the maple trees were just starting to turn ten thousand shades of red and yellow. The pines were deep green, towering high above me. It felt like a church. I walked quietly and tried to keep from thinking about my nightmare. But the memory of it started mixing with my memory of the day before, of lowering Mop's body into the ground. What if my dream was true? What if he'd been alive when we buried him. I tried to be reasonable, to remember how cold his body had gotten, that only the whites of his eyes showed when I pulled open the lids.

As I got closer to the clearing I heard someone talking. And crying. I hid behind a tree where I could have a view of the clearing. Josh Greene was kneeling at Mop's grave!

"Mop, I'm sorry. It's my fault you're dead. I love you, Mop. I'm sorry, sorry . . ." He kept saying it over and over. And crying real hard.

I thought, get away from my dog's grave, you creep. It *is* your fault he's dead. I had to stop myself from running out and beating him up. I'd get him later. When he stood up to leave the clearing I hid in some bushes.

As soon as Josh was gone I went over to the grave and knelt down myself. I listened closely to see if Mop was scratching under the earth. But the only sound was the creaking of a few old pines and the breeze whispering through the maple leaves.

"Mop, Mop, what did I do?" I said. "I should have taken care of you myself."

I sat back on my heels and wondered, where's Mop now? I knew where his body was, but where was his spirit—all the things that made Mop so special and different from any other dog.

I thought of what my mom said when her mother had died. "We all have a little bit of Grandma inside us. We have her spirit—we bring her qualities to the world." I wondered what I had inside of me that was from Mop. His kindness? His sweet nature? His forgiveness? Would Mop want me to blame Josh? To blame myself?

I thought about these questions for a long time. In a way Josh and I had had joint custody of Mop for the last year, the way my mom and dad shared me. If something happened to me when I was at my dad's—an accident like getting hit by a car—would I want my mom to blame my dad? Of course I wouldn't.

"What should I do?" I asked Mop inside me.

And I got an answer.

I'd never been to Josh Greene's house before. I knew where it was though. All the kids did. He lived with his grandmother on the poorest block in town, in a long wood frame building with lots of doors leading to lots of small apartments.

I got there around noontime. Since I didn't know which door led to Josh's apartment or which floor it was on, I asked a lady who was sitting on the steps.

"Third door, third floor," she answered. "Skipping school are you? It'll get you in nothin' but trouble." She pointed to the four little kids who were playing on the sidewalk. "Look where it got me."

"Thanks," I said and headed for the third door.

71

There weren't any doorbells, so I climbed the stairs. I could hear soap opera voices from a TV. It took three times of knocking before Josh's grandmother opened the door. She looked real old and little, all wrapped up in a blanket.

"Yes, yes," she said. She sort of looked at me and sort of didn't.

"Is Josh here?" I asked.

"Yes, yes," she said again. But she didn't move to let me in or turn to call Josh. I looked around her into the living room. The TV flickered but I didn't see Josh.

"When will he be back?" I tried.

"Yes, yes," she said.

Maybe she's deaf, I thought. "When will Josh be back?" I yelled.

"What do you want?" a voice asked from behind me. I turned around to face Josh. He was coming up the stairs with a bag of groceries. "You want to beat me up?" he asked before I could say anything. "Is that going to make you feel any better?"

"No, no. That's not it. That's not why I came. I . . . I . . . want to apologize. I was awful. It's not your . . ."

I stopped because his grandmother was getting upset. She was still standing there, nodding and mumbling, "Yes, yes," louder and faster.

"Can you wait for me?" Josh asked. "I'll be right back."

He put his free arm around his grandmother. "Come on, Grandma. I'll make you some tea."

A few minutes later Josh came out. The first thing I said was, "You cut school, too?"

"Yeah," he said. "I was a coward. I didn't want
72

to face you." He looked me squarely in the eye. "It *was* my fault, Aviva. I took off Mop's leash to play with him. We were sort of wrestling when this squirrel ran by us and across the road. I didn't move fast enough. I never should've taken off the leash that close to the road, I—"

"Josh," I interrupted. "I took Mop off the leash all the time. It could have happened when he was with anyone. I was only blaming you because I didn't know what else to do."

Josh seemed to know what I meant.

We were still standing in the hall. "Do you want to go to the grave?" he asked.

"Yes," I said. "I do." I didn't tell him I saw him there or anything.

"Are you going to make a grave marker?" Josh asked as we walked off his block toward the streets that led to the woods.

"I thought maybe a pile of stones. Something natural," I told him.

"Can I help?" he asked.

"Of course," I said. "We'll do it together."

When we got to the grave site we picked out some rocks from the edge of the clearing. First we put down a large flat gray one, so big it took both of us to carry it. Then we made an arrangement of three small rocks on top of that.

When we'd finished we stood there looking at it. "I wrote a poem," Josh said.

"Let me see."

He pulled a small slip of paper out of his back pocket and handed it to me.

HERE LIES AVIVA'S DOG
MOP
THE MOST WONDERFUL
DOG IN THE WORLD.
SHE WILL MISS HIM VERY
MUCH.   I WILL TOO.

Josh didn't look at me while I was reading it.
"That's real nice," I said as I swallowed back some
tears. "Let's put it under the big stone."

"Do you really want to?" he asked. "I mean Mop's
your dog and everything. Maybe you want to write a
poem instead."

"I like this one," I said. So we put it under the big
flat rock and stood there silently for a few more minutes.

As we were leaving the woods I said, "Maybe we
should have wrapped the poem in plastic, so it won't rot
or anything."

"I like it that way," Josh said. "It will become earth and be part of nature."

"Like Mop," I said.

"Yeah," he agreed sadly. "Like Mop."

By the time we were back on the street it was time for school to be out and I hadn't had any lunch. "I guess I'll go home to my mom's," I said.

When we stopped in front of my house Josh said, "Jackson's going to be furious that we skipped school. What are you going to do?"

I hadn't thought about that. But I figured my mother would understand and write me an excuse note. "Can't your grandmother write you a note or something?" I asked.

"You kidding? She gets confused about stuff. She's sort of senile. I told her today was a holiday. If she knew I cut out she'd be all upset. School's this big thing to her."

"So she's never written a note to Mr. Jackson?"

"No."

"Then I'll write a note for you and make it look like an old lady's handwriting. I can do that."

"You sure?"

"Sure I'm sure," I said. "It'll be in your desk when you get to school tomorrow."

"All right," Josh said. "Let's try it."

We said good-bye. Josh had started running down the block when he turned around and called back, "Aviva!"

"What?"

"Your ankle. You're not wearing the bandage. Is it better?"

For a second I didn't know what he was talking about. Then I remembered. "Yeah. It's all better."

"Good." He was smiling. "We'll beat the eighth grade then."

75

He turned around and kept on going.

I went into the house. There was no Mop to greet me. No wet kisses and yappy, loving barks.

First I had crackers and peanut butter and then I went into my bedroom to write the note for Josh. I bandaged two of my fingers together to make it feel like I had arthritis or something. I was on my third try of "Dear Mr. Jackson. Please excuse my grandson, Josh Greene . . ." when the front doorbell rang.

"Who's that, Mop?" I said out loud before I remembered—no Mop.

I looked through the front window to see who it was. Mr. Sayles, the mailman. So late in the day? And why would he ring the bell instead of putting the mail in the mail box?

"What is it?" I yelled.

He held up a letter. "A registered letter for Aviva Granger," he yelled back.

"That's me!" I said and opened the door. I went out on the porch to sign for it.

Mr. Sayles had heard about Mop from the neighbors. "I'm sorry about your dog," he said. "That was a very nice dog. And believe me, with this job I've seen plenty of dogs over the years. That was a special dog. I'm real sorry."

"Thank you," I said. Everyone was being so nice and I still felt so awful.

As I was going in he added, "Take care of those fingers, now, you hear?"

I looked at my hand still bandaged for writing Josh's note. "Sure thing," I said as I closed the door.

I flopped on the couch and looked at the envelope. It was a soft shade of blue and smelled perfumy. I turned it over to check for a return address.

Cynthia O'Connell
110 Stranton Avenue
Boston, Mass.

George's daughter! I ripped it open.

Dear Avira,

My father just called to tell me that your dog was hit by a car. I'm writing to tell you how sorry I am that your dog has died. I stayed with my Dad at your house, so I met Mop and know what a terrific animal he was.

Even though we've never met I wanted you to know how sorry I am for you. You must be very sad and lonely.

I guess if our parents keep living together we'll meet sooner or later.

Sincerely,
Cindy

P.S.
Thank you for the thank you note you left me at the cabin. You have a nice room too.

I read it over a few times. It was a nice letter. Then George came home with a whole pile of groceries. He was an hour earlier than usual. "I thought you might like company today," he said. I showed him the letter.

"My Cindy's a fine girl," he said after he read it. "You'd like each other." I didn't tell him that's just what my mom said.

George was going to try out a new chicken recipe. "If you don't have too much homework maybe you'd like to help me," he said. Homework? I hadn't even gone to school.

I was cutting up the chicken when my mom called because I had forgotten to call her. Then my dad called to say he'd drop my suitcase off later and why didn't he bring Myrtle, too.

"Sure," I said. "Why not?" At least Myrtle would be someone to talk to after school. "And Dad, you were right. About Josh. It wasn't his fault about Mop."

And I was right about my mom and the note. She wrote a nice "Please excuse Aviva's absence—it was unavoidable" note. As she folded it and put it in the envelope she said, "Next time you feel a need to stay home I want you to talk to me about it before, not after." She was very stern. "Do you understand?"

"Yes." I quickly took the note from her before she changed her mind.

As I walked into Room 416B I was dreading the jokes about Josh and me being absent on the same day. But no one mentioned it. I guess Sue told Rita and Janet and Louise about Mop because they all said how sorry they were. When Sue and I were hanging up our jackets I told her that she was right about Josh, that it wasn't his fault about Mop's death. What I didn't tell her was that we'd both cut school and spent the afternoon together.

When I got to my desk I put my books away and slipped the excuse note into Josh's desk. Mr. J. was writing some questions on the blackboard for History class, but school hadn't officially started for the day so kids were still talking and stuff.

"Miss Granger, your excuse note for yesterday—on my desk please."

"Yes sir."

I brought my mom's note to the front of the room.

He opened it, read it, then looked down at me. "How's your ankle?"

"It's okay now."

"Good. Then we'll beat the eighth grade." Just then Josh walked in. Mr. Jackson turned to him. "Your excuse note, Mr. Greene."

Josh looked at me. I rolled my eyes toward the back of the room.

"Yes sir," Josh said. "Just a minute."

I distracted Mr. J. by asking him what assignments I'd missed while Josh got the note out of his desk. Then we traded places. Josh stood with Mr. J. and I went to the back of the room. My heart was pounding as Mr. J. was reading Josh's note. The bell rang and he put it down to lead us through the Pledge of Allegiance. Another joyous day in seventh grade had begun.

Later, while we were doing our math problems, Mr. J. walked up our aisle and stood between Josh and me.

"Mr. Greene."

He looked up. Mr. J. held up the note I'd written for Josh. "This is a forged note."

Everyone in the room stopped working to listen.

79

"Your grandmother didn't write this note." He turned to me. "Miss Granger, you did."

How'd he know?

He glared at me. I looked at my fingers. "Your own note is authentic, but you forged this one for Mr. Greene. I will call your mother about this tonight. Mr. Greene, you will not go home until your grandmother has come in for a conference with me. You may call her from the office phone during lunch."

"But . . ." I began.

Mr. J. wasn't listening. He was already marching up the aisle booming, "Back to your Math, class."

What was Josh going to do? He probably didn't even have a phone. And no way could his grandmother come in for a conference. She'd get too upset. She might not even understand what was going on.

As soon as the lunch bell rang and we were dismissed I leaned over and said, "I'm sorry, Josh. I don't know how he figured it out."

"He's probably an ex-con who learned all about forgery in jail!" Josh answered angrily.

"What are you going to do?"

He pushed back his chair and grabbed his lunch bag from the floor next to his desk. "Nothin'," he said.

"You mean you're not going to explain or anything?"

He smiled a kind of sad smile. "Nah. Jackson said I can't go home until my grandmother comes. Well, then he'll just have to wait with me. It'll be a regular sit-in."

He laughed and ran to catch up with dumb Cioffi. I sat there for a minute studying my fingernails and getting angrier and angrier at Mr. Jackson.

"Well, Miss Granger. Are you waiting for me?"

Mr. Jackson had come back into the room. We were the only ones there.

"No . . ." I said, then quickly added, "I mean yes. Yes I was waiting for you. I want to talk to you about something." I got up and walked to the front of the room, talking all the time so I wouldn't weaken and run out without telling him what was on my mind. "I want to tell you about why I wasn't here yesterday and why I wrote the note for Josh."

Mr. Jackson sat down at his desk and offered me a seat next to it. But I stayed standing so I could look down on him for a change. I told him about Mop and Josh and how my mother had written a note for me and how Josh's grandmother wouldn't understand. "And," I finished, "I don't think you understand but I thought I'd tell you anyway. If Josh's in trouble, I should be, too. Otherwise you're punishing him for not having a mother, which isn't fair. So I'll stay after school, too."

Mr. Jackson looked me straight in the eye the whole time I was talking and I didn't look away—not once.

"I'm sorry about your dog," he said when I'd finished. "But this is between Mr. Greene and me now. He will remain after school. You will not. Now go have your lunch."

I couldn't tell if he was being mad or nice or what.

I looked for Josh at lunch to tell him what happened. He wasn't in the lunchroom. I hoped he hadn't cut out again and that he was shooting baskets in the gym.

After lunch Josh was back in his seat. The afternoon was pretty normal, except that Josh passed me a note when Mr. J. wasn't looking.

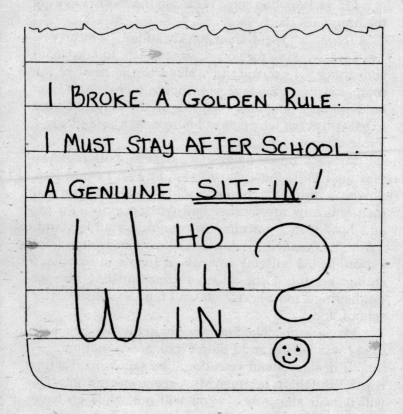

I BROKE A GOLDEN RULE.

I MUST STAY AFTER SCHOOL.

A GENUINE <u>SIT-IN</u>!

WHO WILL WIN?

"Miss Granger," Mr. Jackson said. Had he seen Josh pass me the note? In that instant I decided I'd eat it before I'd let Mr. J. read it out loud. Josh couldn't afford to get in any more trouble. "Read . . . the answer to the third Science question," he ordered.

Mr. J. was slipping!

Eventually the bell rang and school was over. We filed past Mr. J. at his Marine sergeant straightest, each reciting, "Good afternoon, Mr. Jackson." I tried to tell him with my eyes to be understanding with Josh, but a dark brown cold stare was all I got in return.

Maybe I should have taped three fingers together, I thought as I walked home. Or better still typed the note. Why didn't I think of that?

"Hi Mo . . . Myrtle," I yelled when I came into the house. I found her under the couch and gave her a piece of leftover chicken fricassee. The second day after school without Mop was worse than the first. There weren't any registered letters to read, or meals to cook, or phone calls to answer. I tried to do my homework but had trouble concentrating. My brain was filled with thinking about Mop in his grave and Josh and Mr. Jackson sitting in the classroom waiting for a grandmother who would never come. I turned my soap opera on and off about ten thousand times. What was happening to Jason and Eleanor and L.B. was silly compared to the real things going on in my life.

At dinner my mom said, "How are your plans going for your birthday party?" Birthdays? Parties? I'd forgotten all about it.

"I don't know," I said as I stabbed a ravioli with my fork. "I think maybe I'll call it off. I'm not in the mood for a party."

"Mop loved your birthday parties," Mom said. "He would want you to go ahead with it and have a good time. Besides, getting ready will get your mind off your sadness. I don't think you should cancel."

"You don't?"

"I don't."

"Well, I'll think about it," I said.

I left for school early the next day. I wanted to see if Mr. J. and Josh were still sitting there staring at each other. Since Mr. Jackson hadn't called my mom I thought they just might be.

As I turned the corner to school I spotted Josh running across the street to catch up with me.

"What happened?" I asked as we walked into the schoolyard together.

"Whaddaya mean, what happened?"

"Come on. With Mr. Jackson."

"Nothin'."

"What do you mean nothin'?"

"We shot some baskets. That's all."

"Come on, Josh. About the note and your grandmother? How long was your sit-in?"

"I told you, we shot some baskets and then Mr. Jackson gave me a ride home. He said if I couldn't bring Grandma to him he'd bring himself to Grandma."

"Oh, no!" I moaned. I could just picture Mr. Jackson getting Josh's grandmother all upset.

"He was cool," Josh said. "He didn't tell her I cut out or nothin'. Just what a good kid I was and how much potential I have."

"Really?"

Josh slid against the building and sat down. "Really," he said. "Cross my heart and hope to . . . Well, anyway it's true. He even offered me a . . ." Josh hesitated.

"Offered you a what?" I sat down next to him.

"Job. He offered me a job."

"Doing what?"

"I'm not going to take it though. I wouldn't."

"Doing what? You didn't tell me what job you're talking about."

"I told you it's nothin' cause I'm not going to do it."

"You have to tell me, Josh. What does he want you to do?"

Josh picked up a stick and broke it in half. He didn't look at me when he said real low, "Walk his dog. But I'm not going to do it."

My heart thumped. I tried to keep from feeling mad or sad. Josh wanted to be a veterinarian for goodness sake. Walking dogs was a great job for him. And I was the only one who could tell him it was all right for him to do it again.

"Don't be silly," I said. "You should take it."

He looked up at me. "I don't know. It's not right."

"It *is* right. You're a good dog walker."

By then loads of kids were in the schoolyard. The last thing I needed was for Janet or Rita or Louise to see me with Josh Greene. So I split quick and went into school.

Sue came in right after me. "You still going to have your party?" she asked when we were in the cloakroom. "I mean after Mop. Everyone wants to know. I said I'd ask you."

"Sure," I said. "I'm still having the party, if you're still helping me."

Sue's face lit up like a neon sign. "Great," she said. "I'll come over to your house after school and help. Okay?"

"Okay," I said. I was glad there'd be someone around the house besides Myrtle and me.

When I got to the back of the room there was a folded piece of paper on my desk. I turned to the back wall and opened it.

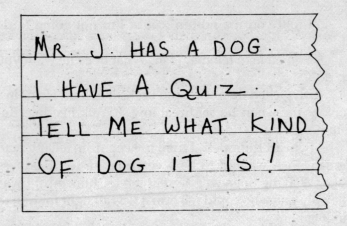

MR. J. HAS A DOG.
I HAVE A QUIZ.
TELL ME WHAT KIND
OF DOG IT IS!

I looked around for Josh. He was horsing around with dumb Cioffi in the cloakroom. I thought for a minute and looked at Mr. J. at the board—six feet two and all muscles. Then I sat at my desk and wrote under Josh's quiz.

a.) A Great Dane

b.) A Doberman Pinscher

c.) Both of the above

I put the note on Josh's desk. Just before the bell rang Josh came back to his seat and opened the paper. He read my answer and shook his head no.

"A German Shepard?" I whispered.

He shook his head no.

My heart sank when I asked, "Not a sheepdog?"

He looked at me. "Oh no," he said, sort of shocked.

I looked at the clock. The bell would ring in ten seconds. Josh pretended to be getting an assignment from his notebook. I punched him on the arm and hoped no one would see. "Tell me," I hissed through my teeth.

The bell rang. Josh handed me back the paper. On the bottom he had quickly scribbled, "A miniature poodle."

This is how you keep from laughing during the Pledge of Allegiance. With great difficulty.

"So what are you going to wear?" Sue asked. We were sitting at the kitchen table eating popcorn and making a list of snacks and drinks to buy for the party.

Wear? I hadn't thought about what to wear. But since we weren't going to be in costumes I'd have to figure something out. "I don't know. What about you?"

Sue loves clothes and her mother is a real homebody mom who makes things for her. Real up-to-date fashions. And she'd done it again. "My mother made me a dress just for your party," she said. "She copied it out of a magazine picture I showed her. I'll bring the picture to school so you can see it." Then she remembered it was *my* party. "Maybe your mom'll get you something new," she said.

When? I thought. My party's Saturday. Today's Tuesday. Mom works until five every day. Sue must've read my mind (best friends are like that) because she said, "The shopping center's open Thursday nights. Get her to take you then."

"Yeah, maybe then. All I have is sweatshirts and jeans."

"What about that pretty blue and white dress from last Easter, with the gray pumps?"

I looked down at my expanding chest and my size eight-and-a-half, still-growing feet. "Nothing from last year fits."

"Aviva," Sue said when I was walking her to the door.

"Yeah?"

Her eyes were filling up with tears. "I miss Mop, too."

CHAPTER NINE

My
Party!
S   29

FROM THE SECOND I OPENED MY EYES, THE DAY OF MY
birthday party was busy, busy, busy, and full of sur-'
prises.

The first surprise was a bright blue angora sweater
draped over the footboard of my bed. It was the one I
liked best when Mom and I went shopping on Thursday
night. The one she said was too expensive! Now it was
mine.

The second surprise was that I got my period for the
second time. Sister Bernard Marie said some girls aren't
regular at the beginning. They have it once and then not
for a few months. But not me. There it was on the day of
my birthday party.

The third surprise was a phone call from George's
daughter. I took the phone from George and sat on the
couch.

"Happy birthday, Aviva. This is Cindy." Her
voice was soft, feminine—like the smell of her writing
paper.

"Yes, I know. Thank you for the letter . . . about
Mop. It was nice."

"You're welcome. My dad said you invited loads of
kids to your party. Do you have a lot to do to get
ready?"

"Not too much—just move some furniture and decorate. This is the first year we're not wearing costumes or doing trick or treat," I said.

"We're having a costume party in my dorm. If I feel better this afternoon I'm going to put something together."

See, I thought. You don't get too old for costumes. Rita and Janet didn't know anything.

"Are you sick?" I asked.

"Just my period. I have bad cramps on the first day."

"Me too. Not cramps." I was embarrassed, but once I started I had to finish. "I mean, my period. I got it today, too."

Cindy wasn't embarrassed at all. "What a coincidence. That happens you know—roommates . . . and sisters—sometimes end up having their periods in sync."

"Really?" Mom and Sister Bernard Marie didn't tell me that.

"Uh-huh. We're kind of funny roommates though. Don't you think? I mean we've never met. We use the same rooms, only at different times."

I didn't know what to say.

"Anyway, Aviva. I have to go. I just wanted to wish you a happy birthday."

"It's really Monday," I said. "But everyone's celebrating Halloween today because of school and everything."

"Well happy birthday Monday."

"Thanks."

"Maybe the next time I'm in town we can get together. I'd like to meet you face to face. My dad says you're a great girl."

"He did? That's what he says about you."

"He does?" She sounded surprised.

"Yeah. All the time."

As soon as I hung up the phone it rang again. Without even saying hello first, my dad sang "Happy Birthday To You" in three languages—English, French, and Gaelic (because my mom's family is Irish). "We'll celebrate on Monday with a Chinese dinner," he said. "Maybe the waiter will sing it in Chinese."

In the afternoon George went out on a secret mission. Another surprise? Right after he left, Sue came over to help move furniture around so we could dance in the dining room. We also strung up long ribbons of orange and black crepe paper and put out bowls of Halloween candy and chips and stuff. My mom baked a big cake. She put orange food coloring in the frosting and outlined a jack-o'-lantern face on top of the cake with black jelly beans. Since it was my twelfth birthday she made a "12" for each of the eyes. It was a pretty weird-looking cake.

About six o'clock—an hour before the party—Sue left and I went to take a shower and get dressed. Just as I got out of the bathroom and back into my room, I heard a commotion in the living room.

"Put it there," my mom said.

I strained to listen more closely.

"Let's cover it with a sheet," George said.

"Where is she?" Josh asked. Josh?

"Getting dressed," my mom answered.

And I did—get dressed—as fast as I could.

"Aviva," my mother called. "Hurry up. There's a present out here waiting for you."

A present? That George and Josh gave me together? Please, I prayed. Please don't let it be another dog. I'm not ready to love another dog. Tears came into my eyes as I pulled my sweater over my head.

I took a deep breath, put on a smile, and went into the living room. The first thing I saw was Josh—in a real shirt, with a collar. And loafers instead of sneakers. "Hi," he said. "Happy birthday."

"Hi," I said back. "What's going on here?"

He pointed to a big box shape, about five feet square and covered with a sheet. "It's your birthday present." Please no dog, I prayed again.

George, a big grin spread across his face, stood next to it. "It's from Josh and me, but it was Josh's idea."

"Yeah. But you paid for it," Josh said.

"But you did most of the—" George was saying when Mom interrupted him.

"Enough already. Let her see it before she faints from suspense." She smiled at me as she got up from the couch. "Pull off the sheet, honey."

I grabbed one end and gave a tug as I prayed one more time, no dog. Not yet.

My prayers were answered. It wasn't a dog. It was Myrtle in the most wonderful, zany turtle house ever. It was a deep wooden box with a ramp leading to a sunken pool made with a pan. And on the outside of the box there was colorful writing and drawings, by Josh of course.

"It's wonderful," I screeched. "It's just wonderful." Before I knew it, I'd given George a big thank you hug. Of course I didn't give Josh one. "Thank you—both," I said.

Then I knelt down to read the rhymes. They had that Josh Greene ring. Like:

92

ROSES ARE RED

VIOLETS ARE PURPLE

THIS IS THE HOUSE

OF MYRTLE THE TURTLE!

We carried the box into my room and filled the pan with water. Myrtle climbed the ramp and dropped into the pool. Then she looked up at Josh and me with a satisfied smirk and sank to the bottom for a rest.

Just as Josh was making me promise not to tell the other kids about the present the doorbell rang. Josh jumped nervously. "See ya later," he yelled as he ran toward the kitchen.

"Where are you going?" I called after him.

"I'm not going to be here when the gossip gang comes in," he called over his shoulder. "That's for sure." The back door opened and closed and Josh was gone.

Rita and Janet and Louise came first. Then Sue—in her new dress—followed by the other regulars. Not one eighth-grade boy had come by seven-thirty. Neither had Josh.

We had sodas and stuff and played music real loud. But nobody danced or talked that much. If we had on costumes, I thought, at least there'd be something to talk about.

The doorbell rang. I went to open it. Finally two eighth-grade guys—the cutest, Bob and Sammy—were standing there with Josh and Cioffi. Sue's eyes lit up when they walked in. Everyone perked up.

"So, so," Bob said as he looked around. "Where's the action?"

Josh checked out the place as if he'd never been there before. "Looks like a pretty dull party to me."

"Played any games yet?" Bob asked.

Rita grinned at him knowingly and sort of whispered, "Not yet. Wait until her mother goes for the pizzas."

Oh no, I thought. Games? *Kissing* games? I'll die. I hate them—hate them. I mean I wouldn't mind kissing a guy if he was my boyfriend or something. But just any guy, like say, Cioffi. Ugh!

Ten minutes later my mom and George went for the pizzas.

Josh and Cioffi thought spin-the-bottle was a great idea, probably because the eighth-grade boys thought of it. And everyone else went along, including me.

Rita gave the orders. "Okay, everybody, sit in a circle."

We all sat down on George's puke green rug. Bob put an empty soda bottle in the middle and went back to his place in the circle. "Where's the kissing room?" he asked.

"Kissing room?" Rita shot back.

"Oh, I forgot," Bob said. "You're just seventh graders. The real way to play spin-the-bottle is to go into the kissing room and kiss while we all count out loud to twenty."

"Of course," Rita said, like she knew all along when we all knew she didn't. "Aviva's room will be the kissing room." She'd love a twenty-second kiss with Bob, I thought.

"So who spins first?" Cioffi asked.

Bob looked at me. "The birthday girl."

Everybody looked at me.

"Oh, no," I protested.

"Oh, yes," everybody answered.

I should have called my party off, I thought, as I knelt next to the bottle.

"What if it points to a girl?" I asked.

"Then you spin over again, silly, until you get a boy," Louise said, making sure everybody knew she knew everything there was to know about kissing games.

I did a quick count. There were nine girls in the circle. Maybe I'd get one girl after another and by then my mom would be back.

Girl, girl, girl, I wished as I gave the bottle a spin.

It spun and spun and stopped. It didn't point at a girl. It pointed at . . . *Josh Greene!*

Some kids clapped. A couple shouted, "Yea." Rita said, "The bottle never lies."

Josh jumped up and said, "Let's get it over with." We went into my room and closed the door.

Josh put his hands in his pockets and let out a deep breath as he started pacing. He was looking anywhere but at me. "What jerks!" he said.

I checked on Myrtle. She was still sleeping at the bottom of her pool. I'd sure love to change places with you, Myrt, I thought.

"Okay," Rita's voice rang out. "Start when we say 'one.' "

"This is dumb," I said.

95

"The dumbest thing ever," Josh said as he looked down at Myrtle.

He lifted her out of the water. "I'd rather kiss Myrtle," he said.

"So would I," I answered.

"One," they yelled in unison.

We grinned at each other and both planted kisses on Myrtle's shell. Myrtle looked from one of us to the other with as confused an expression as a turtle can manage.

"Two . . . three . . . four . . ."

This is what it's like to kiss a turtle for twenty seconds. Better than kissing a boy.

P.S.
We beat the eighth grade 46–42.

| Aviva Granger | 18 points |
| Josh Greene | 16 points |